BACKSHOOTERS STALK SLOCUM!

Slocum saw the shadowy forms of two people—most definitely his assailants—pressed flat against the brick tenement. Another shot rang out, hitting the cobblestone six inches away. Slocum decided there was enough of the gunner visible now to make his move, though it would mean exposing himself. Not that he had any choice—his attackers had him pinned down good.

Slocum leaped up and squeezed off three shots. He heard a cry of pain, then saw someone fall into the garbage-strewn alleyway . . .

SPECIAL PREVIEW!

Turn to the back of this book for an exciting excerpt from the blazing new series . . .

DESPERADO

DON'T MISS THESE
ALL-ACTION WESTERN SERIES
FROM THE BERKLEY PUBLISHING GROUP

THE GUNSMITH by J. R. Roberts
> Clint Adams was a legend among lawmen, outlaws, and ladies. They called him . . . the Gunsmith.

LONGARM by Tabor Evans
> The popular long-running series about U.S. Deputy Marshal Long—his life, his loves, his fight for justice.

LONE STAR by Wesley Ellis
> The blazing adventures of Jessica Starbuck and the martial arts master, Ki. Over eight million copies in print.

SLOCUM by Jake Logan
> Today's longest-running action western. John Slocum rides a deadly trail of hot blood and cold steel.

JAKE LOGAN

SLOCUM AND THE FORTY THIEVES

BERKLEY BOOKS, NEW YORK

For W. G.

SLOCUM AND THE FORTY THIEVES

A Berkley Book / published by arrangement with
the author

PRINTING HISTORY
Berkley edition / April 1993

ISBN: 0-425-13797-X

A BERKLEY BOOK ® TM 757.375
Berkley Books are published by The Berkley Publishing Group,
200 Madison Avenue, New York, New York 10016.
The name "BERKLEY" and the "B" logo
are trademarks belonging to Berkley Publishing Corporation.

PRINTED IN THE UNITED STATES OF AMERICA

10 9 8 7 6 5 4 3 2 1

SLOCUM AND THE
FORTY THIEVES

1

"Whiskey," Slocum told the bartender. "And leave the bottle."

The bartender nodded and slammed a bottle of rotgut down on the mahogany bar, then put a shot glass down beside it. The glass—much like the man who was about to use it—hadn't seen anything resembling clean water in weeks.

Slocum flipped one of his two remaining silver dollars onto the bar and poured a healthy slug into the glass. The stuff felt like a river of fire sliding down his gullet. Slocum mentally calculated that he'd just consumed about half his life savings; another three drinks would exhaust it completely.

Not that John Slocum was worried about where his next meal was coming from. Women, meals, and money always had a way of taking care of themselves.

Slocum coolly eyed the Kreeg brothers from across the saloon. Both were playing poker with a couple of locals; Harley Kreeg was dealing off the bottom, while his brother Elvin distracted the suckers with wild yarns about his days with Quantrill.

Brushwood Gulch, Colorado. Slocum had arrived an hour earlier, determined to end it with the Kreegs that same afternoon. He'd been tracking them from Salina, Kansas, where the Kreegs had robbed the First National Bank, killing a teller and a deputy sheriff in the process. The robbery was the culmination of a monthlong spree in which the Kreegs had robbed, raped, and murdered their way up from St. Joe, Missouri to Denver.

After the posse came up empty handed—the Kreegs seemingly had vanished somewhere near the North Fork— the marshal in Salina promised Slocum a thousand dollars for each of their heads. Trouble was, the marshal wanted the Kreegs brought in alive, so that the good people of Salina might have the pleasure first hand of watching Harley and Elvin get their scrawny necks stretched like warm taffy.

Dead, the Kreeg brothers were worthless.

Slocum took inventory: except for the Kreegs, their suckers, the bartender, and a short Oriental man drinking beer at the end of the bar, the place was empty. An ancient grandfather clock in the corner wheezed out two gongs.

It was just a matter of time before one or both of the suckers would catch Harley cheating, and then the fun and mayhem would begin. Harley would deny it, of course, and Elvin would back him up. "You callin' my brother a cheat?" Elvin would ask indignantly, jumping up, whipping out the firepower. From there, the lead would start flying. Slocum had seen dozens like the Kreegs and knew their routines inside out.

With the prospect of any pain-in-the-ass innocent bystanders getting caught in the cross fire at a minimum,

Slocum was about to make his move on the Kreegs when he felt a tap on his shoulder.

"Buy an old Texas Ranger a drink, friend?"

Slocum turned to see a grizzled old coot with a scraggly white beard and a nose like a plump cherry tomato. Slocum thought of a Santa Claus who'd fallen on hard times.

"Get your sorry ass out of here, Jug, Jackson" the bartender snapped, "or I'll take the back of me hand to you."

"You and who else, peckerwood?" Jug challenged. He grabbed a clump of Slocum's shirt and pulled him close, surprisingly forceful for an old man. He motioned to the bartender. "Time was, I'd've put him on a spit and et him for supper. Though right now I'd settle for one of them *aperiteefs*. Wouldn't mind one of them pickled eggs, neither—"

A chair crashed into the wall. Elvin Kreeg was up.

"You callin' my brother a cheat?" Elvin's hand hovered close to his holstered Remington .44. Not a great weapon, but good enough for short distances.

Slocum sighed. Like the weather, some things never changed. His odds had just gone down the crapper, thanks to the old geezer. He tossed his last silver dollar onto the bar. "Give the old man what he wants," he said, his eyes never leaving Elvin Kreeg. He took a few steps toward their table.

By this time, one of the poker players was also scrambling to his feet, reaching for his gun. Slocum stopped abruptly, his fingers gliding over the business end of his Colt. With any luck at all, this hayseed might actually mortally wound one of the Kreegs, and the bounty would be reduced by half.

Slocum was about to order Elvin to drop it when a voice from behind saved him the trouble.

"Hold it right there, Kreeg."

Slocum looked to his right. The voice belonged to a stocky man with a tin star pinned on his vest. Doubtless the Kreegs' reputation was common knowledge even in Colorado.

Harley Kreeg, still seated, grinned, his mouth a corncob pecked clean. Elvin's right hand inched away from his holster. He raised his arms in the air.

You're dead, lawman, Slocum thought, seeing the sheriff from the corner of his eye.

A shot rang out; Slocum saw Harley clutching his six-gun under the table, a puff of smoke rising from the barrel. Slocum gulped; he hadn't even seen Harley's hand move. He saw a red spiderweb forming on the sheriff's white shirt. Harley had gotten him half an inch above the heart. The rifle dropped from the sheriff's frozen hands and he crumpled to the floor of the saloon.

"Mighty fine shootin', Harley," Elvin said, relaxing.

Harley holstered his gun. "Weren't nothin', little brother," he said. "Like geese in a barrel."

"Best we take our winnings and move on," Elvin suggested.

As the other two townie poker players watched, totally cowed, Elvin swept up the ill-gotten gains into his hat.

John Slocum found his chance to make the bounty. He peeled off two shots that ricocheted between Harley's legs, an inch below his sweetmeats.

"The party's over, boys," Slocum said. "Drop those barking irons. There's some people in Salina who want to get to know you a whole lot better."

Harley glanced at Elvin and reached for his gun at the same time. Not soon enough: Slocum's ebony-handled Colt Navy was already out and spitting lead. He'd aimed carefully for Harley's shoulder, but the bastard ducked and the first bullet ended up dead center in Harley's forehead. There was still enough life left in him to squeeze off one good shot at Slocum. It grazed Slocum's ear and landed harmlessly in the grandfather clock.

Elvin Kreeg quickly trained the barrel of his gun on Slocum's gut and was about to fire when a second shot rang out and blew off half of Elvin's jaw. Elvin's eyeballs rolled up into his skull and he folded to the floor like a sack of snakeshit.

"Never could abide a backshooter," Jug said behind him. He stuffed his six-shooter into the back pocket of his baggy pants.

"Guess I owe you a drink," Slocum said to the old man. He made his way over to the sheriff, where a dark red pool of blood had puddled under his midsection.

"Get the doc," Slocum said to the bartender.

"Save your breath, Slocum," the sheriff said, a bubble of blood on his lips. "I'm finished."

"Just rest easy, friend," he said as he cradled the dying man in his arms. "How'd you know my name?"

"Every lawman knows you, Slocum," the sheriff said, his breathing labored.

By this time, some of the townsfolk were crowded around the door to the saloon. The town doctor pushed his way through the mass of bodies and crouched down beside the sheriff. Slocum couldn't help but notice the bottle of rye whiskey among the surgical tools and bottles of pills as he opened his black bag.

"Where does it hurt, Ben?" the doc asked, but the sheriff waved him away with dwindling strength.

"Hurts when I breathe, you worthless old sawbones," Sheriff Ben Webster croaked. With great pain, he grabbed Slocum's arm.

"I took your bullet, Slocum," he said. "You were hunting them, weren't you?"

"Guess I was," Slocum said.

"Then you owe me one," Webster said, swallowing hard.

"Name it," Slocum said.

"Brushwood Gulch is a good town, with good people . . . mostly." Webster glanced over at a pudgy middle-aged man dressed in a business suit. "You got to make me a promise." Webster's face was the color of Swiss cheese. "I remember when you rode shotgun for Wells Fargo. Heard you took on Onions McGee and his gang single-handed. Gonna need a man such as yourself to keep the peace here."

"You mean be the sheriff of this one-horse burg?" Slocum asked.

"What the hell you think I mean, dimwit?" Webster coughed, producing a fine spray of blood. "I know your kind, Slocum. You ain't the type to deny a dyin' man his last wish. This territory's got a ways to go before it's completely civilized. Promise me you'll keep an eye on Brushwood Gulch, at least 'til you can find another lawman as good as yourself."

"You overestimate me, Sheriff," Slocum said. Now that the Kreegs were finished and the two-grand bounty was dust in the wind, it was time to stake out a new claim, and Brushwood Gulch didn't seem to hold many opportunities.

"Do it, Slocum. I'm counting on you." Webster coughed again, his face a mask of pain. His eyelids flickered twice and then shut tight.

Don't you die on me, you old bastard, Slocum thought angrily.

"And don't forget to put some flowers on Nellie's

grave every now and then," Webster sputtered, coming to life again.

"Who's Nellie?" Slocum asked.

"My ex-wife. Lives over to Chesterton."

"Lives? How can I put flowers on her grave if she ain't dead?" Slocum asked now.

"I was kinda hopin' you'd kill her for me," Webster said. His eyes flickered and he died again. This time Slocum knew it was for keeps.

"Shit," he muttered.

Slocum retired to the bar and poured himself a healthy slug. The Kreeg brothers were already drawing flies. There was nothing he wanted less than to be the sheriff of Brushwood Gulch, but at the same time, he knew that the tin badge would be adorning his vest before nightfall. Every man had his own code, and Slocum's would not allow him not to honor Webster's last wish.

"Terrible, just terrible," a pudgy man said, wiping his fleshy brow with a hanky as he bellied up to the bar. "Give me a bourbon, Ned," he said to the bartender. Some of the townspeople were already removing the dead bodies; their stoic faces told Slocum they'd been through this many times before.

Slocum busied himself rolling a cigarette. He knew what was coming.

"Damn shame," the pudgy man said, downing his bourbon. "Webster was a fine lawman. Served us well for over six years. Now the good people of the Gulch will be easy prey for every prairie rat and all-around reprobate who sees fit—"

"Do I know you?" Slocum asked.

"Horton Everett at your service, sir," the pudgy man said, sticking out a ham hock of a hand. "I'm the mayor of Brushwood Gulch. Also dabble in the banking trade."

Slocum decided not to accept the handshake. "How can I help you, Mr. Everett?"

"Heard Ben's dying wish, Mr. Slocum," Everett said. "A real man wouldn't think twice about offering his services."

"Better find yourself a real man then," Slocum said, wanting to pour himself another but knowing he was broke.

"Job pays twenty-five a month plus room and board," Everett said.

"Not interested," Slocum said.

"Of course, for the right man, the town might be willing to go as high as thirty."

"Still not interested," Slocum said.

"How about fifty a month, with the room and board of your choice?" asked a sultry female voice.

Slocum slowly turned to see a heavily coiffed, buxom brunette of probably 25 to 28 years old with a 36- to 40-inch bosom formed by no less than the Almighty Himself. They were tantalizingly squeezed together in a tight gingham dress like two cozy cantaloupes. She wore too much makeup—Slocum wondered briefly if she applied it with a cake decorator—but even without it she would have been a knockout.

"Don't believe we've been introduced," Slocum said, his eyes glued to the woman's twin assets.

"Folks call me Midnight Rose," the woman said, "and I'm *not* in the banking business. Of course, for a man like you, I may be able to see my way clear of taking your personal deposits."

"Not now, Rose," Everett said, clearly flustered. "Mr. Slocum and I are conducting—"

"Tell me more, Miss Midnight," Slocum said.

"I run the finest and cleanest house this side of Denver,

Mr. Slocum," she said. "As sheriff of this town, you would be afforded certain privileges *non grata.*"

Slocum couldn't help but notice four very attractive young ladies of the evening—or in this case, ladies of the afternoon—congregating behind Midnight Rose. All were as heavily made-up as Rose and wore the same seductive smiles. Brushwood Gulch suddenly looked somewhat better.

"Can I sleep on it?" Slocum asked.

"Alone or with company?" Midnight Rose countered.

Slocum glanced over at two men who were about to lift Webster's lifeless body. "Hold it right there," he said, and pointed to Webster's tin star. He turned to Mayor Everett. "Keep that badge handy. Let me study on your offer a bit."

"Yes, yes, of course, Mr. Slocum," Everett said, a gleam in his eye. "Take all night to decide."

2

Slocum couldn't quite remember the last time he'd been served a sumptuous meal in bed. Come to think of it, he'd *never* been served a meal—sumptuous or otherwise—in bed.

And what a meal it was: a one-pound beefsteak broiled and seasoned to perfection, candied yams, and crisp French fried potatoes. After subsisting on hardtack for the last three weeks while stalking the late, unlamented Kreeg brothers, Slocum devoured the meal ravenously.

At the end of the bed, Midnight Rose sat and expertly clipped his overgrown toenails. Supper in bed was her idea. And nothing less than her own bed, a silk-sheeted, perfume-scented King Edward imported all the way from St. Louis, would do.

They were on the third floor of Midnight Rose's Good Time Saloon and Emporium. It was pushing nine o'clock on that Saturday night, and already the joint was in full swing. Down in the bar, the strains of a honky-tonk piano could be heard amidst a chorus of drunken cowpokes singing, brawling, and faro playing.

"Judging from the length of these toenails," Midnight Rose said, clipping off another, "I'd guess you've been on the trail going on a month."

"Twenty-four days to be exact," Slocum said, wiping the last of the gravy with a piece of bread, a kind he had never seen before. It was round, somewhat coarse, and had black seeds in it. "What kind of bread is this anyway?"

"Rye bread," Midnight Rose said. "I have it imported from back east, New York City."

"You send all the way to New York City just for bread?"

"Only when I get homesick," she said. "Have enough to eat?"

Slocum belched loudly. "Reckon I have."

"Good," Midnight Rose said. "Don't take this personally, but your bodily odor leaves something to be desired." She reached over and yanked a thick cord next to the bed. As if by magic, the bedroom door opened and a rotund Negro woman appeared.

"Virginia, would you be kind enough to draw a bath for Sheriff Slocum?"

"Yes'm, Miz Rose," Virginia said, and left.

"I ain't decided to be the sheriff yet," Slocum said.

"We'll see," said Midnight Rose.

Slocum felt his manhood begin to stand at attention as Midnight Rose squeezed the sponge between his shoulder blades, sending a stream of warm, soapy water down his back. He was sitting in a porcelain bathtub, hairy knees folded almost to his chest. Up until this evening, he would never have been caught dead in a bubble bath; now he was grateful for the soap bubbles. They hid the sight of his rapidly stiffening member.

"Bubba Chin told me all about your shootout with the Kreegs," Midnight Rose said, rubbing the sponge all over Slocum's chest now.

"Who?"

"Bubba Chin," she said. "He runs Bubba Chin's Chop Suey Palace down the street. It's the only Chinese restaurant west of Kansas City. He was in the saloon when the shootout happened."

Slocum remembered an Oriental man who'd been drinking at the bar. "You mean the tiny chink?" he asked.

"The tiny *Oriental,*" she corrected. "We don't tolerate prejudice of any kind in Brushwood Gulch."

"You're white, what do you care?" Slocum asked.

"I care because I've felt many times the sting of prejudice," she said. "Being Jewish and all."

"Jewish? Really?" Slocum asked surprised. "Can't say as I've ever actually met a real Jew before."

"Don't worry, we don't have the devil's horns," she said acidly, pulling back her dark curls.

Slocum grinned. Here was a woman who would give him a run for his money, if he'd had any. He grabbed the back of her head and pulled her down so that their lips were almost touching.

"Kiss me, devil woman," Slocum said, his tongue already out and quivering like a divining rod.

Instead, Midnight Rose tore away and cracked Slocum so hard across his left cheek it left his ears ringing. Almost simultaneously she reached down into the murky bathwater and grabbed his cock, holding it in a vise-like grip.

"Watch your manners, Mr. Slocum," Midnight Rose said, her angry expression reminding Slocum of a marauding Comanche.

"Whatever you say, Miss Midnight," Slocum said with a sickly grin.

She loosened her grip; then to Slocum's surprise she planted her plump red lips firmly against his, her tongue forcing its way between his teeth and halfway down his throat, or so it felt like. Just as quickly she broke the kiss and started in with the sponge bath again.

"It's not Miss Midnight," she said, unfastening the first three buttons of her corset. "It's Miss Liebowitz. Rose Liebowitz, from Rivington Street. That's on the Lower East Side of New York, where I was born."

"How did a pretty little New York Jewess like yourself end up in this God-forsaken hellhole?" Slocum wanted to know.

"You don't know what hell is, Slocum, until you've lived in New York," she said. "Shoved in a tiny room, your only heat what comes out of a rotten little stove, nothing to eat but onions and stale bread and smelly old sardines. Every now and then there'd be potatoes, but they were usually rotten.

"A hundred people in our building shared one outhouse," she went on. "You want diseases, New York's got a full menu of them. Dysentery, malaria, measles, chicken pox, mumps, tuberculosis. If one of those doesn't kill you, there's always the thieves, murderers, rapists, and every other scum of humanity to contend with. When you've got fifty thousand people trying to live in six city blocks, there's going to be problems."

"Only takes one man to stop a riot, or so the Texas Rangers say," Slocum said. "A little law and order can change a man's disposition right quick."

"Save your breath, Slocum," Rose said. "I've seen plenty of your type since I came west. Roll into town with a full bankroll and leave with a hole in their pocket, that is, if you don't leave without a hole in your head first."

Slocum sank deeper into the bathwater. "Just no getting on your good side, is there?" he asked.

"There's always a way for a man to get on my good side, Slocum," she said, and took his hand. "I think you're as clean as any man can be." Slocum stood and stepped out of the tub.

Rose led him back into her boudoir and gently eased him down onto her bed, her green eyes softening as he started hardening again. She climbed atop him, straddling him, and then unbuttoned the rest of her corset so that her well-rounded breasts flopped before him in wondrously full view.

God, I love women, especially when they're naked, Slocum thought.

"We need law in this town, you handsome jerk," she said. "And I need a man who knows what to do with his trigger finger."

Slocum knew that Midnight Rose was using her alluring charms to persuade him to become the new sheriff in Brushwood Gulch. He thought of his daddy's words: "Never let any woman lead you around by your dick, John Slocum, else you'll never have a moment's peace."

"I got four of the finest whores west of the Mississippi working for me, Slocum," Midnight Rose said, stroking his penis, "and if you deal yourself into this round, you can work your way through them at no cost."

"Starting with you?" Slocum wanted to know.

"Starting with me," she said.

Slocum licked his lips and cupped her firm tits in his hands then gently squeezed her rosebud nipples. She let out a barely audible gasp of pleasure, rubbing his chest. Slocum pulled her down just close enough so that her plump breasts were half an inch from his mouth. He hungrily took her left nipple into his mouth and sucked deeply on it until it became hard. He repeated the process with the other nipple. Midnight Rose, in the opening stages of passion, clutched his head tightly to her heaving bosom.

Slocum's mouth found hers, and they kissed deeply. Her tongue slowly slithered into his mouth like a rattlesnake exploring a gopher hole. Slocum circled his arms around her and drew her down so that she was pressed flat against his chest. His hands traveled down to her plump buttocks, and he lovingly caressed them. His cock was pulsing with anticipation, pressed flat against her frilly bloomers. Clearly, the fact that she was still half-dressed presented a problem. Not for long, though.

"Slide under the covers, Slocum, while I disrobe," she whispered.

Slocum did as instructed, and seconds later Midnight Rose slid into the bed beside him, as naked as the day she came into the world.

Slocum rolled on top of her and feasted on her luscious mounds once again, sucking her nipples until they turned dark pink. Her breathing quickened and she moaned in anticipation of his love.

Slocum sensed her hunger and obligingly plunged his erect penis deep into her velvety snatch. Midnight Rose met him halfway, thrusting her hips so that she greedily swallowed up his manhood. She wrapped her legs around his waist and held on for the ride.

Slocum grabbed her ass cheeks and started pumping her, their bodies locked together in a sweaty embrace. Midnight Rose rubbed the soles of her feet against his legs and gently bit his earlobe. She had yet to meet any man who didn't respond to the earlobe maneuver. Though it had been some time since she had taken a customer herself—she preferred to handle only the administrative end these days—she still had a few tricks up her sleeve.

Slocum continued thrusting in and out of her, trying to hold off his own climax for as long as possible. Unfortunately, it had been nearly a month since he'd had a woman, especially one as willing as Midnight Rose. His weakening resistance matched her growing passion, and he was helpless to hold back much longer. Her silky smooth womanhood, tight and hot, clenched his cock with no intention of letting go.

Slocum moaned deeply and exploded deep inside of her, filling her with his steaming seed. Midnight Rose embraced him tightly, her own climax not far behind. Together they rocked in the throes of ecstasy as their orgasms peaked and then slowly subsided.

Sweat dripped off of Slocum's brow as he completed the job, his climax ebbing into a fading memory.

"Miss Rose, I just want to say," Slocum said, rolling off her, "that you're the tightest little thing I've had all day."

"You got one hell of a bedside manner, Slocum," Rose said, and walloped him with a pillow. Slocum saw that she was grinning from ear to ear.

Another day, another doll.

Slocum munched on a piece of angel food cake, getting crumbs all over the bed. Midnight Rose sat propped up against the headboard next to him, rolling him a smoke. Slocum marveled at how skillfully she assembled the cigarette, and told her so.

"In this business," she said, giving it one last lick, "you learn everything that pleases a man."

"Just how *did* you get into this business?" Slocum asked her.

Midnight Rose popped the cigarette into Slocum's mouth and struck a match on the floor, bringing the flame up and lighting it.

"My father was a tailor by trade," Midnight Rose said, "and after my mother died in a smallpox epidemic—I was twelve at the time—he decided he'd had enough of the slums and the dirt and the disease. We packed up and headed west, got as far as Fort Smith, Arkansas, where he found work. We settled there, and six months later he died of consumption." She shook her head ruefully. "They say the Lord works in funny ways, but frankly, I didn't get the joke.

"There was a woman in Fort Smith, Jewel Moon. Maybe you've heard of her mother, Temperance? Jewel ran the fanciest whorehouse in the region. By this time I'd turned thirteen and was, let's say, very well developed for my age.

"Jewel stood five feet three inches, and weighed more than two hundred pounds—every ounce of it hard muscle. She was one tough bird. But fair. Never tried to cheat any of us girls out of our share. One of her customers was a wealthy Jewish merchant named Abram Jacobson. He took a real shine to me."

"I can understand that," Slocum said.

Midnight Rose nodded and went across the room to a maplewood bureau, where she pulled out a bottle of expensive brandy and two glasses. She poured them each a healthy shot.

"Abram was well into his sixties when we met," she continued. "We were 'conducting business', as Jewel used to say, when he expired in my arms. Seems Abram had a weak heart and knew his days were numbered. At least I assume he did, because he left me ten thousand dollars in his will."

Slocum whistled softly.

"I decided to go into business for myself," she went on. "But Jewel didn't want the competition. So I headed further west, ended up here in Brushwood Gulch, and started my own establishment."

"Looks like you've made a success of it," Slocum said.

"I can't complain," Midnight Rose said, and downed her brandy, then poured herself another. "I still travel back east every now and then. I have a lot of friends and relatives in New York. I hope to return there someday and live in style. Once an easterner, always an easterner.

"In the meantime though," she said, refilling Slocum's glass, "I have to admit that Colorado—Brushwood Gulch especially—has been good to me. I like this town, Slocum. It's a good town, with good people. I want to keep it that way, and I need your help."

"I already told your mayor I'm not interested in being the sheriff," Slocum said. "The only life I'm interested in protecting is my own."

"You haven't heard my offer yet," she said.

"Yes, I have," he said, "and as alluring as your girls are, I don't let my manhood dictate my actions. Thanks, but no thanks."

"I'm offering you, in addition to the salary the town pays you, ten percent of the gross profits from my establishment. I'm also confident that I can persuade the other businesses in town to kick in as well."

"Not interested," he said, and paused. "How much would that be?"

"Brushwood Gulch can put seven hundred dollars in your pocket each and every month."

Slocum tried to hide his astonishment but failed as his eyebrows raised up an inch. Midnight Rose moved in for the kill.

"Let me put it to you this way," she said. "We need law and order in this town. The kind that will tame this territory. Make it civilized."

"Like New York City?" Slocum asked, not without a hint of sarcasm.

"Don't get haughty," she said, hitting him on the arm. It hurt. "Colorado is a different kind of wilderness. I saw you in action today, Slocum, and I liked what I saw. We need your brand of justice . . . and I'm willing to go as high as twelve percent."

"Could you see your way clear to fifteen percent?" He smiled, knowing he was pushing her, and enjoying it.

"Thirteen and a half," she said. "Don't be a *schmuck,* Slocum. Where else can you get that kind of money for what you do? Unless you *want* to spend the rest of your life hunting down vermin like the Kreeg brothers. What do you get per head for those *shmendricks,* twenty-five dollars? Fifty if they're wanted in more than six states, nothing if you have to kill them?"

"It's a living," Slocum said defensively.

"Of course it is, and I respect that," Midnight Rose said. "Let me ask you a question: how many nights this month have you slept on a goosedown mattress?"

"Well—"

"And how many nights in the last two years have you spent on the prairie when you started to think a sheep might be good for more than wool?"

"Hey, I don't—"

"And how much did you have in your pocket when you rolled into town today?" she asked. She was smiling, but her eyes were granite.

"Money's never been that important—" he started to say, but Midnight Rose forged ahead, not even listening.

"Looking at you," she said, "I would say you're a man who's long seen the ass-end of forty."

"Ass-end of forty my butt—"

She went on, oblivious to his protests. "There's always a new breed of outlaw, always someone younger, a little quicker on the trigger. Oh, you still drill them, but it's getting tougher. Nowadays, you're content to get them half an inch lower in the heart than you used to. You think, maybe I'm gettin' to be a few years past my pistol-packin' prime. But you keep on going, because it's all you've ever known."

Slocum opened his mouth to speak, he couldn't think of any words that seemed appropriate. This gal could take the wind out of a man's sails faster than a fart in a blizzard.

"I'm offering you more than you've ever had, or will ever get, Slocum," she said. "I'm making you the finest offer you're likely to receive for doing what you're *already* doing for a tenth of the price."

Midnight Rose, still naked as a jaybird, flung herself on top of Slocum and kissed him deeply.

"Think about it, Mr. Bigshot," she said. In her hand was the tin star.

"Where'd you get that?"

She merely grinned. He grabbed the badge, intending to pin it on his chest when he remembered he wasn't wearing anything to pin it on. "You got yourself a deal."

"Now that we've settled that," she said, rolling off him, "here's *our* requirements: I don't want a single shot fired on Saturday night unless it's from *your* gun."

"Agreed," Slocum said.

"Any strangers come into town, they check their guns with you . . ."

"Agreed," Slocum said.

"Any poor drunk bastard you throw into jail, I want him out five A.M. so we don't have to feed him any bacon and eggs . . ."

"Agreed," Slocum said.

"Any hardcase you have to kill, we don't want to smell his stinking carcass the next morning . . ."

"Agreed," Slocum said.

"If you have to hang him, the price of the scaffold comes out of your cut . . ."

"Don't push your luck, little lady," Slocum said.

Midnight Rose smiled now, and caressed his leg.

"Can you start tonight?"

"For fifteen percent I can," Slocum said.

"I'll do my best with the town council," Midnight Rose said, and started fondling his member.

Slocum had no doubt that she would.

3

Sunday morning, Slocum got a break. Except for Jug Jackson sleeping off a bender in one of the cells, the jailhouse was free of prisoners.

The Brushwood Gulch sheriff's office was pretty much like any other west of the Mississippi. Wanted posters dotted the wall behind the sheriff's desk—including two for the Kreeg brothers. Slocum ripped them off the wall and used Harley's to light a cheroot.

There was a pot-bellied stove in the middle of the room with a rusted coffeepot on one burner. Slocum peered inside; all that remained were the dregs of Ben Webster's morning brew. Slocum looked for some wood to start a fire and make a fresh pot. Coffee would help keep him awake. He needed it—especially after his nearly all-night session with Midnight Rose.

"If you're lookin' for some wood," said a voice from the cell, "Webster kept it in the back. And make it snappy. It's gettin' a mite chilly in here. Got one foot in the grave already." Jug was full awake and full of beans.

"Not likely," Slocum said, slightly amazed to see Jug conscious, considering all the rotgut that'd flowed through his veins. The last Slocum had seen of Jug Jackson, the town character, was when he had parlayed Slocum's silver dollar into all he could drink. Not too tough, since Slocum had instructed the barkeep to let Jug drink his limit, courtesy of John Slocum. It wasn't every man who saved his life.

"Don't suppose there's anything like a deputy in this town?" Slocum asked.

"You're lookin' at him," Jug said, sitting upright on the bunk.

"You kidding?" Slocum asked. "I need a deputy who can stand up straight and not wobble for at least ten hours a day. Not some old drunken tosspot who can't be relied on."

"Relied on me plenty yestiddy," Jug said indignantly, scratching his balls. "Weren't for old Jug Jackson, you'd have the gophers deliverin' your mail now."

"Can't argue with that," Slocum agreed. "How much are they payin' you for your deputizing?"

"Nothing," Jug replied.

"Then I'll double it," Slocum said. "Now fetch us some wood."

"What I meant was, I wasn't the deputy before, but I am now, 'cause Lord knows, you look like you need all the help you can get."

"Thanks for the vote of confidence," Slocum said, "reckon I may be needing some help though. I'll give you your meals, a bed to sleep in, and some pocket change so you can get a snootful whenever you're off duty. And I mean *off* duty."

"I'll take ten percent of whatever you're stealin' from the town merchants," Jug said.

"Five percent," Slocum countered, "and no drinkin' *at all.*"

"Make it seven and a nip now and then," Jug said.

"Make it mostly *then,*" Slocum said, "and you got yourself a job."

"I'll get some wood," Jug said, going into the back room where he started throwing wood chips into a box. "What say we drink a toast to our new working relationship?" he called.

"Ain't got a bottle," Slocum called back, dumping the coffee dregs into a wastebasket.

"Try the bottom drawer in the desk," Jug replied. He started tossing coal into the stove.

Slocum pulled open the drawer; sure enough, a bottle of Old Panther, seal unbroken, lay atop some ancient, yellowing papers.

"Webster always had a bottle handy," Jug said, firing up the stove now. He struck a match against his stubbled cheek. Slocum had never actually seen anyone do that.

"Mighty accommodating of him," Slocum said. "But didn't I just hear you make a promise to me regarding your consumption of spirits?"

"Call it an advance against services rendered," Jug said, licking his lips as Slocum poured out two stained glasses of the hooch. The coffee could wait. Jug pulled up a chair and curled his hand around the glass in the same motion.

"Luck," Slocum said.

"Luck," Jug repeated, and they both knocked back their drinks.

"Allow me." Jug poured them each another. They repeated the process.

Twenty minutes later, a little more than half of the bottle was gone. Slocum felt relaxed and well oiled. So far, he liked the job and the citizenry of Brushwood Gulch.

"Don't let this go to your head," Slocum said to Jug. "You saved my hide yesterday, and I'm grateful."

"Do the same for me someday and we'll be even," Jug said.

They clinked glasses and drank to it.

Two hours later saw Slocum and his new deputy roaring drunk. They'd sung every song they each knew about the Almighty and and had moved on to old songs about horses, towns, and women. Jug then went on to an old ditty he called "Kentucky Song," about a pioneer wife. He sang, "Remember that land of delight/Is surrounded by Comanche who murder at night./Your house they will plunder and burn to the ground,/While your wife and children lay murdered around." Jug didn't get a chance to finish though, because right in the middle of the first chorus a tall, thin, pasty-faced man stormed into the office and started babbling about some crazy cowboy who was rip-roaring drunk and threatening to shoot up the town.

"Slow down, Norman," Jug said to the man. Norman was the widow Jones' half-wit son who ran things at the town stable. "Wipe that drool off your chin and tell me what's going on."

"It's Henry Harper again," Norman said, his Adam's apple bobbing up and down. "Says his brother Cyrus saw Henry's wife and John Bryson check into the hotel together and he's gonna blow 'em both into the hereafter even if he has to shoot up half the town to find 'em."

Norman wasn't exaggerating. Two shots rang out down the street and they heard the sound of shattering glass.

"There goes Mister Entenman's bakery," Jug said.

Two more shots rang out, followed by a woman's blood-curdling scream.

"Tell me about this Henry Harper," Slocum said, his words coming out slightly slurred. He realized that he was piss-drunk, and wasn't relishing the thought of facing down a local hothead.

"Nice enough when he's sober, meaner than a rattle-snake when he's been drinkin'," Jug said. "And right about now, I'd say Henry's about twelve sheets to the wind."

A moment later two more shots rang out, shattering the window of the dry goods store. This was followed by a drunken war whoop from Henry Harper.

"He's heading for the hotel all right," Jug said.

"That's six shots," Slocum said. "Best time to make your move is when they're reloadin'."

Slocum stood somewhat unsteadily and put his hand on the swivel chair for support. Not a smart move, he knew at once, as the force of his weight caused the swivel chair to slide across the wooden floor. Slocum fell ass-backwards, and would have caused his spine serious damage had Jug not been there to catch him.

"You're gonna have to do a whole lot better than that, Slocum," Jug said, shaking his head sadly.

"Let free of me, you old turkey-neck," Slocum slurred. He shook himself free and headed for the door. "You be the town character and I'll be the law."

When he was halfway out the door, Jug called out to him.

"Henry Harper's pretty handy with a gun, drunk or sober. Try not to get killed first day on the job."

His back still to Jug, Slocum said, "Ain't no man ever got the drop on John Slocum, and no man ever will." Whiskey always made Slocum somewhat pompous. "I've tamed a million Henry Harpers in a million cow towns and 'spect I'll have to tame a million more before the West is safe for decent folks."

Slocum, fortified by some ninety-proof rotgut, strode confidently out the door when Jug called out to him again.

"Before you get to a million and one, lawman, you might need this." He tossed Slocum's gunbelt across the room—it hit him square in the butt.

Slocum stopped dead in his tracks and felt his face turning a dark shade of red. Purple would be next.

He bent slightly and grabbed his gunbelt. "You're gonna make someone a fine wife someday," he mumbled at Jug.

Sure enough, Henry Harper's world was spinning even faster than Slocum's, as evidenced by his feeble attempts to reload his six-gun. Henry was on his hands and knees, trying to locate dropped bullets. Sitting beside him was an almost full bottle of whiskey. Henry successfully loaded one bullet, then another. Slocum moved—some might have said staggered—toward his quarry.

"Henry Harper," Slocum called out, "drop your gun and—"

Harper squeezed off a shot at one of the six blurred Slocums he saw; unfortunately, he chose the one in the middle, which was the real Slocum. Fortunately, Harper's aim was off just enough so that the bullet flew harmlessly over Slocum's head.

Slocum quickly returned the firepower. His aim, as it turned out, was also off—it missed Harper's left foot by a good four inches and merely kicked up a little dust.

"Hop it, Drarper," Slocum attempted to say. The words refused to come out right. He was drunker than he thought. "A Slocum don't mish twishe."

"In a pig'sh ash," Harper drunkenly replied. He fired at Slocum again. Slocum's luck held; Harper missed— again, barely—and his third shot was the harmless click of an empty cylinder.

Slocum weaved unsteadily toward Harper who was back on his hands and knees, looking for more bullets. As he reached out for one, Slocum stepped on his hand.

"Le'sh talk, Henry," Slocum slurred.

"Go screw a buffalo," Harper said, and punched Slocum in the balls. Slocum doubled over, but not before the toe of his boot connected with Harper's chin, sending him sprawling into a mound of horseshit.

Harper was quick; Slocum had to give him that. He scrambled to his feet, however unsteadily, in seconds. Along the way he'd grabbed the whiskey bottle and swung it in Slocum's direction.

Slocum grabbed Harper's arm in mid-swing. "That'd be a terrible washte of good whishkey, Harper."

"Ah, screw it," Harper said, and sank to the ground. He pulled the cork from the whiskey bottle and took a healthy swig. "Bitch wasn't worth the prishe of a postage stamp anyway." Harper then burst out crying.

"Oh, don't take it so hard, Harper," Slocum said. He sank to the street next to Harper, who blew his nose into his sleeve and handed Slocum the bottle. "She ain't the only head in the herd."

"Couldn't cook for shit," Harper sniffed. "Bishkits tashted like gunnysack. Never washed my jeans nor ironed my shirts nor gave me the pleasure a man expesh from his woman." This brought a fresh round of tears. Harper blew his nose again and took the bottle from Slocum. "But damn if I shtill don't love her."

They continued drinking in the middle of Main Street. Harper poured his heart out, and the whiskey poured down both their gullets. There they sat until the whiskey ran out, drunker than two saddletramps after a six-week drive.

They were buddies now. Harper threw his beefy arm around Slocum's shoulders and said, "You know, Shlocum . . ."

"Yesh?" Slocum said.

"I wash jusht thinkin' . . ."

"What?"

Harper's mouth opened but his words were nowhere to be found. He attempted a second time to speak, and failed.

"Hell with it," Harper said, and promptly passed out.

Slocum looked at Harper's unconscious form. Harper was already snoring contentedly.

"Now don't thish beat dying?" Slocum asked him, and also passed out.

From the second floor window of the whorehouse, Midnight Rose and Mayor Everett watched the comic spectacle. Everett was a regular, though his tastes in women ran to big-hipped Swedes.

"Hope we made the right choice," Everett said, doubt in his voice.

"We did," Midnight Rose said with a smile.

4

Slocum devoured the fried chicken, string beans, two baked potatoes, biscuits and gravy, and an eight-inch slab of blueberry pie, washed down by three steins of beer, two shots of whiskey, and a pot of coffee, all courtesy of Midnight Rose's Negro cook, Jennie Mae, who delivered three sumptuous meals a day to the jailhouse.

Slocum pushed himself away from his desk, fully sated, and belched loudly. He lit a fat cigar and puffed contentedly, patting his belly. From the feel of it, he'd gained approximately five pounds in the one week he'd been the law in Brushwood Gulch. The town definitely agreed with him. So did Midnight Rose, for that matter.

Her guarantee of unlimited credit at her whorehouse went unused by Slocum. Truth of the matter was, he was kind of stuck on Midnight Rose, and he was pretty sure she felt the same way. Nothing had ever been said between them, but actions spoke louder than words. Though the town council provided him with living quarters above Brannigan's dry goods store, he spent six nights a week in Midnight Rose's bed. On the seventh day he rested.

Word around the territory was that John Slocum was firmly holding the throttle of the law in Brushwood Gulch—and God help any misguided bastard who rode in looking for trouble.

All in all, things around town were pretty quiet. Thus far, Slocum had only been called upon to quell four barroom brawls, remove a dead horse from behind Ed Pinkney's barber shop, and chastise six-year-old Suzie Creamer for cheating four-year-old Dougie Lucas at jacks.

Slocum smoked and thought about the future. He wanted to hate the joys of contentment. He knew that a man who was totally happy, whether by the love of a good woman or something like a new saddle, was apt to become soft, easy prey for the first hardcase rat with a Colt and a bad attitude.

Jug, sitting on a cot in one of the cells, polishing his rifle, read Slocum's thoughts. "Kinda liking it here, ain't you, Slocum?"

"Yeah, and it scares the bejeezus out of me," Slocum said. Outside, Main Street was quiet enough to hear a bird blink. "If I had half an ounce of brains I'd clear out. My bones hate it when I stay in one place for too long a spell."

"Don't fight it, Slocum, life is too short," Jug said. "I oughta know. Had my own share of pretty ladies in my day. If I'd had one as pretty as Midnight Rose, chances are I'd have stuck with her for the long haul."

Midnight Rose sashayed through the door with a picnic basket on her arm. Even Slocum had to admit that she looked happier than a hungry buzzard circling a dead rabbit. Her cheeks were a healthy pink, while the rest of her face seemed suspended in a permanent smile.

"Just thought you boys needed a snack," she said cheerfully, dropping the basket on the desk and circling her arms around Slocum's waist.

"We just finished supper three minutes ago," Slocum said, liking the way she felt against him.

"I also haven't seen my honey-man in two hours," she said.

She kissed Slocum passionately, then pinched his nose. "You're the cutest little *bubby* I've ever seen," she squealed delightedly, then turned and seemingly floated toward the door. "Don't forget, Slocum: Sundown. My room. Be there or I'll be gunnin' for ya."

She giggled and disappeared into the dust of the late afternoon.

"I do believe I'm in love," Slocum said, watching her cross the street, her shapely behind swaying rhythmically.

" 'Spect so," Jug said.

Mayor Horton Everett paid them a visit that same afternoon. He was a small man, maybe an inch or two over five feet tall, a fleshy gnome in an expensive brown tweed suit. In addition to being the mayor, he also owned the First National Bank of Brushwood Gulch. Like all bankers, he was a thorn in John Slocum's side.

Everett wiped his sweaty brow with a yellow-stained handkerchief. "Good day, Slocum," he said. He looked worried.

"Good day, Mayor Everett."

"I have a problem," Everett said, getting right to the point. "It's that Ike Griffith. He hasn't made a payment on his farm in four months and, I'm sorry to say, I must foreclose on the mortgage."

"What's that got to do with me?" Slocum asked, already knowing the answer.

"As the sheriff of Brushwood Gulch, one of your duties is to—"

"Seems to me," Slocum said, "Ike Griffith has three young'uns and a mother-in-law to keep fed."

" . . . as the sheriff of Brushwood Gulch is to uphold the laws . . ."

"And you want me to be the bearer of the bad news?"

"Don't get me wrong, Slocum," Everett said. "I don't enjoy this one lick, but as president of the bank . . ." He pulled an official-looking paper with fancy red seals on it from his breast pocket. "It's your job to serve this notice."

"And if I refuse?" Slocum wanted to know.

"I'm afraid refusing is not an option to one in your position, Sheriff," Everett said.

He handed the foreclosure notice to Slocum, who knew it was useless to argue with the beady-eyed banker. He took the paper and stuffed it in his pocket. It was, Slocum knew, one of the more unpleasant aspects of his job.

"Where do I find this place?"

"Fifteen miles to the northeast," Everett said. "And I want Griffith and his family off that spread by tomorrow. Counting on you to see it gets done, Slocum. Good day, sir." With that, Everett was gone.

Slocum sighed, headed for the stable to get his horse, and told Jug not to expect him back until dinnertime.

"Goin' to chase the Griffiths off the land they been sweatin' bullets over for nearly ten years?" Jug wanted to know.

"Don't suppose you'd want to do it for me, seeing how you're so cozy with them and all?" Slocum said.

"Can't get cozy with a riled rattlesnake, and that's what Griffith's gonna be when you hand him that paper," Jug said. "Besides, you ain't payin' me enough for that, Slocum," he added, pouring himself some coffee. "Treat you to a cup of brew before you head out though."

"No thanks," Slocum said grimly. "I better get moving if I want to get there and back before sundown. Just do me a favor and don't put nothing stronger in that coffee than cream and sugar, at least 'til I get back."

"Don't worry your bowels in an uproar, Slocum," Jug said. "I'm a changed man since I found the Lord Jesus."

Slocum had to ask. "And when did the likes of *you* find the Lord Jesus?"

" 'Bout nine-thirty this mornin' when Doc Lockhart told me my next drink might be my last." Jug made a sour face. "Reckon I've given my liver a right solid beatin' over the years and it's time to make amends to it."

"That ulcer juice you're swilling there'll do you just as bad," Slocum said.

Jug raised his coffee cup in a mock toast. "I'll drink to that."

Slocum grunted and made his way to the stable. Norman Jones was already mounting up Slocum's chestnut.

"She all set to go, Sheriff Slocum," Otis said. "Mr. Everett come by personal-like and tole me to get yo' horse ready."

Slocum had guessed as much. "How kind of him," he said.

He slid one foot into the stirrup and mounted, then headed toward the Griffith place. He was not looking forward to the task that lay ahead.

Slocum saw the wagon heading his way. It was brightly colored—blue and red, with a few dashes of yellow. It had just topped the horizon and, at that distance, it was hard to tell where one color stopped and another began. As it got closer, Slocum knew those hues indicated that it belonged to either a circus or a traveling medicine show. Circuses

were bad enough; thieves, scoundrels, rapists, even murderers were known to travel with them. Medicine shows,
Slocum knew, were even worse; some of those spellbind-
ing pitchmen could dazzle a man into drinking his own
piss and make him think it was French champagne.

Whatever they were, Slocum wanted them nowhere
near Brushwood Gulch.

When Slocum and the wagon were about an eighth of
a mile apart, he turned his horse sideways so that they
were standing lengthwise in the middle of the road. A
clear challenge.

The wagon drew closer, and Slocum saw that his second
hunch was right on the money. The paint on the wagon
seemed a trifle faded, but the black lettering on either
side was clear enough: "Castleberry's Miracle Purplebark
Sarsaparilla Elixir Emporium."

Manning the two-horse-drawn wagon were a couple of
the sorriest, scurviest, and meanest looking mugs Slocum
had seen in quite a spell. One was short, squat, and looked
like he hadn't seen the sharp end of a razor since last
Thanksgiving, not that he was the type you'd want to
share any cranberries with. The other was tall, lean, and
had a jagged scar that ran from his left eyebrow down to
his lower jaw. Even at a distance, Slocum saw that his eyes
were lifeless black dots, all-knowing and mistrusting.

"Help you, gentlemen?" Slocum asked as the wagon
drew to a stop. The badge pinned to his vest gleamed in
the midday sun.

"We ain't breakin' no laws," said the short, squat one.
He spit a dark stream of tobacco juice a foot from the
chestnut's hoof. On closer examination, Slocum saw a
small white feather dangling from his right ear. Slocum
guessed that a small hunk of tar was probably holding the
feather there.

"Didn't say you was."

"Then let us by."

"Where might you boys be heading?" Slocum asked.

"Don't imagine that's any of your damned business," said the tall one, and Slocum knew at once that these boys were Yankees. Their Eastern accents were thicker than a side of bacon and their demeanor arrogant and self-assured enough to indicate nothing but.

"I'm afraid I have to disagree," Slocum said, the tips of his fingers sliding over the butts of his six-shooters. The fat man had a pretty impressive Colt Dragoon holstered at his pudgy side; Slocum saw his hand inching slowly toward it.

Slocum was already drawn and shooting the white feather off Tubby's ear before the fat man could even go for his gun. Slocum was aiming his second shot for the man's thick gut when the curtains covering the wagon's opening parted. A dapper, nattily dressed man of about forty stepped through. His black hair was heavily greased and combed back. He had a neatly trimmed goatee and a moustache that curled up at either end. He had a white towel draped around his neck, and his face was half covered with shaving soap. Even before the man opened his mouth, Slocum knew he was probably slicker than snot on a doorknob.

"Gentlemen, gentlemen," the man said, revealing a gold front tooth. "What seems to be the problem here?" He looked at Slocum's star.

"Don't much like your man's attitude," Slocum said. "That's the problem. You in charge here?"

"Jedadiah Eustace Castleberry at your service."

"Slocum, John Slocum, sheriff of Brushwood Gulch," he said. "Ever been there?"

"Unfortunately, I have not yet had the opportunity to

visit your fair burg," Castleberry said smiling, toweling off his face.

"I'd be obliged if you kept it that way," Slocum said.

"We were planning on merely passing through," Castleberry said, still grinning. Slocum had never trusted people who grinned for no reason. "Denver is our ultimate destination."

Slocum said, "Up yonder a mile you'll find a fork in the road. Go left and you'll shave twenty miles off your trip."

"I do appreciate the advice, of course," Castleberry said, "but according to my map, your would-be shortcut will actually *add* twenty miles to our trip."

"It wasn't a request, Mr. Castleberry," Slocum said.

"Then might I take it as a threat?" Castleberry asked.

"You can take it as the law."

Castleberry stroked his goatee thoughtfully. "Well, Sheriff," he said, "inasmuch as we are not wanted men, nor have we broken any laws, from a legal standpoint—"

"Save your breath, Castleberry," Slocum said. "I know what you're carrying in the wagon, and I don't want no poison-peddlin' snake oil salesmen killin' half my town."

"Ah," Castleberry said. "You are obviously under the mistaken impression that we are selling a bogus product and you feel that you must do as your conscience dictates. However, I should point out that Doctor Castleberry's Miracle Purplebark Sarsaparilla Elixir contains no harmful ingredients whatsoever."

Castleberry made his way down off the wagon and walked toward Slocum, gesturing with his hands as he spoke. "Yes, I am well aware that there is a legion of unscrupulous, scurrilous vermin crawling around this territory, hawking their deadly wares to an unsuspecting citizenry, and they've tarnished the reputations of honest and hardworking men of medicine such as myself to the point we are viewed with anything but trust."

Castleberry turned to his traveling companions.

"Joshua," he said to the fat one. "Kindly hand me a bottle of the fruit of my labors."

Joshua reached into the wagon and pulled out a bottle of Castleberry's swill. Unlike the other bottles in the crate, this one had a red cork. Castleberry kept it handy for situations such as this; pain-in-the-neck lawmen often frowned upon his product, which contained—among other things—sixty percent wood-grain alcohol. The bottle Joshua handed to Castleberry, who in turn handed it to Slocum, contained nothing more than sugared, colored water with a mixture of cinnamon, spearmint leaves, and oil of cloves.

Slocum uncorked the bottle and sniffed its contents. He took a tiny swig. No doubt about it—the stuff was free of alcohol.

"See?" Castleberry said. "Made only with the ingredients the good Lord saw fit to bestow upon us." Castleberry grinned again, as though he and Slocum were enjoying a private joke. "Of course, I *did* add a small dash of extract of imported Peruvian coca leaf for a little kick, all perfectly legal, of course."

"Uh huh," Slocum said, not impressed. "Mind if I sample another bottle, one you haven't doctored for my benefit?"

Castleberry's ever-present grin vanished for half a second, but reappeared just as quickly. From the corner of his eye, Slocum noted Joshua and the other mug also seemed slightly panic-stricken, as they looked helplessly to their boss for guidance.

"I'd be more than happy to honor your request, Sheriff

Slocum," Castleberry said, "but most unfortunately, what you hold in your hand is our very last bottle. We're on our way to Denver, where shipments from all over the globe are awaiting us so we can replenish our stock."

"Then you won't mind if I see for myself." Slocum holstered his pistol and climbed off his horse, never taking his eyes off Joshua and his co-worker.

"As you wish," Castleberry said, and turned away from Slocum just long enough to pull out a derringer that he'd hidden under his belt. He turned back to Slocum and fired once, catching him in the back as he dismounted. The bullet missed his spine by a fraction of an inch and lodged under his right shoulder. Slocum fell to the ground. The chestnut galloped off in fright.

Slocum lay motionless in the middle of the road, blood seeping from his wound.

"Jesus, boss," Joshua said, prodding Slocum with a booted foot. "You can't kill a lawman in Colorado and not get hanged. When they find his body—"

"Shut your blowhole, stupid," Castleberry snapped, his cultured tone giving way to his Hell's Kitchen origins. "They'll not find his body after we make it disappear. Unfortunately, we don't have the time to chop him up and dump him in the Hudson River like we did to Waterfront Charlie last year."

Castleberry scanned the surrounding countryside. "Throw him down the ravine and let the buzzards have him. By the time he's found we'll have already fleeced the territory and we'll be safely on a train back home to New York."

Joshua kicked Slocum onto his back, and said to Castleberry, "Should I check for a heartbeat, boss?"

"Have you ever known me to miss?" Castleberry asked, his eyes hard.

"N-no, boss," Joshua stuttered. He'd angered the boss by questioning his aim, and angering Castleberry had proven fatal to many a foolish man along New York City's waterfront. "I w-was j-just—"

Luckily for Slocum, who was still very much alive though unconscious, Castleberry's pride would not allow him to believe his target had been anything but a bull's-eye. A second shot, even as a precaution, would weaken him in the eyes of his helpers.

"Do what I said and let's get the hell out of here," Castleberry ordered.

Joshua and Henry, the tall one, dragged Slocum to the side of the trail, then heaved him off an embankment. Slocum tumbled down the side of the ravine and disappeared into a cluster of thick brush.

"Gone, as if by magic," Castleberry said.

He turned to his companions in crime.

"Brushwood Gulch awaits us, gentlemen," he said. "Let's make some money."

5

"I was a man with one foot in the grave," Castleberry cried, standing on a rickety stage before his wagon as fifty of the good people of Brushwood Gulch innocently hung onto his every word.

"I suffered from the ravages of diseases such as rheumatism, rickets, and a host of other maladies too numerous to mention for the faint of heart," he went on. "And to think—me, a graduate of the Harvard School of Medicine, stricken in his prime by the very illnesses I was trained to eradicate. But modern medicine proved ineffective, and I was forced to concoct my own remedies if I were to survive.

"I consulted with the most learned herbology experts from the Far East, with monks from Tibet, whose holistic practices are responsible for prolonging the lives of the high priests—"

Deputy Jug sauntered through the crowd, eyeing Castleberry and company suspiciously. He pushed his way through the throng of people to the front.

"According to ordinance thirty-one, paragraph seven-

teen of the Brushwood Gulch charter, y'all are required
by law to have your peddler's license visible at all times,"
Jug said, proudly showing off the deputy badge pinned to
his chest.

"Very true, my friend," Castleberry said, not missing
a beat. "However, I am a medical practitioner, not a
common peddler."

"Then let me see your medical license," Jug said.

"Very well. Never argue with the law," Castleberry said
graciously. Castleberry stuck his hand through the curtain
of the wagon. In his line of work, this request was not
uncommon. Henry, the tall one, was there, slapping a
rolled-up parchment into Castleberry's waiting hand.

"Which one is it?" Castleberry whispered to his assis-
tant.

"Harvard," Henry whispered back. "Like you said in
your speech."

Castleberry unrolled it and held it up for the crowd
to see. "Here you have it ladies and gentlemen. Harvard
Medical School—class of eighteen hundred sixty-six, further proof that Dr. Jedadiah Eustace Castleberry knows of
what he speaks . . . Let it be known here and now that I am
a man who heals . . . not steals. Yes, ladies and gentlemen,
I hold in my hand—" He reached for a bottle of the
amber-colored liquid. "Castleberry's Miracle Purplebark
Sarsaparilla Elixir, good for whatever ails you: aches and
pains, rheumatism, gout, poor blood circulation, whatever.
Suffice it to say that my miracle elixir has proven effective
in eight out of ten patients, all of whom have praised me.
People whose lives were a living hell are now enjoying
heaven on earth."

He pulled a bundle of letters from his jacket pocket and
started reading one.

" 'Dear Dr. Castleberry,' writes Mrs. Alice McCord of

Cincinnati, Ohio. 'The good Lord saw fit to plague me with dizzy spells, a faint heart, and blood that refused to flow down to my feet. My health was so poor that my husband was certain he'd finally be shut of me forever. Happy he was, too, until I started using your Miracle Purplebark Elixir. In less than three days, my cheeks were rosy red, my heart was beating stronger than ever before, and my blood was flowing like the headwaters of the Mississippi. I even had enough strength to leave that old buzzard of a husband. Thank you, Dr. Castleberry, for giving me back my life.' "

A hushed silence had fallen over the crowd; even Jug was mesmerized. Castleberry knew they were sniffing the bait; a good sign. Now it was time for them to swallow the hook.

"Make no mistake, good people of Brushwood Gulch," he went on. "My elixir is so valuable that several major drug companies tried to purchase it for enormous sums. I rejected all offers, knowing that they would exploit my life's work and charge exorbitant prices for it, stealing the precious pennies of hardworking Americans. Yes, ladies and gentlemen, like the Devil himself, they tried to tamper with my soul. When I still refused, these greedy, Yankee charlatans actually attempted to kill me, thereby burying my formula with me, the same formula that was capable of putting them out of business. Oh, they offered to let me relinquish my secret formula in exchange for my life and would have no doubt killed me had I refused. But the Lord Jesus was in my corner, ladies and gentlemen. I managed to escape their evil clutches and ever since I have devoted my life to spreading the Lord's greatest gospel—Castleberry's Purplebark Sarsaparilla Elixir."

"We've had snake oil salesmen slither through town before," Jug said. "All had tongues smoother than velvet, but they was still peddlin' poison."

"You doubt my word, sir?"

"I doubt the word of every sneaky, low-down, side-windin' pissant too lazy to make an honest dollar," Jug said, crumpling the diploma and dropping it into the muddy street.

Castleberry knew this was a crucial moment; the crowd could turn on him like a rabid dog at any moment.

"You sir," Castleberry bellowed at Jug, "are a man who fears death!"

"Everybody fears death," Jug said.

"Exactly," Castleberry said, "but you display your fear of death by spitting in its eye. Instead, dear sir, you're spitting in the eye of good health by ignoring the symptoms of a weak body!"

"Balls," Jug said, an element of doubt in his voice.

"Well, sir," Castleberry said, moving in for the kill. "I would say just by looking at you that you suffer from acute gallstones, perhaps a weak heart, and maybe a liver dysfunction brought on by a steady diet of beans, bacon, and bourbon."

"He got that right, Jug," said a man in the crowd.

Castleberry uncorked a bottle and handed it to Jug.

"Drink deeply the nectar of good health, my friend," Castleberry said.

Jug raised the bottle to his lips, then hesitated and shoved it back at Castleberry.

"You first," Jug said to him.

"But of course," Castleberry said graciously. He took the bottle and brought it to his lips. However, just as he was about to drink, Joshua hobbled into view. He was supported by a crutch, limping badly and looking generally wretched. Castleberry jerked the bottle from his lips and held it out in Joshua's direction.

"There!" Castleberry cried, indicating Joshua. The crowd turned to look at this pathetic-looking man in their midst. "There is a man who needs this bottle more than I. Come, sir. Drink and be healed."

"Ain't no medicine kin cure what ails me," Joshua whimpered, playing his part, as always, to utter perfection. Castleberry felt a tinge of pride. Joshua O'Grady had been a featured player in Abner McGonigle's Traveling Shakespeare Company and had been fired in Muncie, Indiana for drunkenness and for smashing Othello's head to a bloody pulp with a chair. The two actors had been fighting over Desdemona, a nineteen-year-old ingenue named Molly Stufflebeam who couldn't act but rather got her job by sleeping her way through half the company. Like Castleberry, Joshua O'Grady was a rough-and-tumble native of New York's violent West Side and didn't much care whether he earned his living honestly or not. Right now, O'Grady was using his two talents—play-acting and thievery—to their best possible advantage, stealing both the show and the audience's money.

"There is now a medicine that can help you," Castleberry told him.

"In a pig's ass!" O'Grady called back, and twenty good Christian women gasped in unison. "I tried everything and my leg's still dead."

"I would not insult the obvious intelligence of these fine people by claiming that one single bottle of my elixir will cure you on the spot. It takes time and patience to sow the seeds of good health. Time and my tonic. Drink my good friend, and feel the blessing of Castleberry's Miracle Purplebark Sarsaparilla Elixir."

O'Grady considered it for a minute, then shrugged and said, "Might as well, got nothing to lose."

He hobbled to the front of the crowd and took the

offered bottle. "I'm warning you though," he said, "this leg's good for nothing but show. Cavalry doc in Virginia wanted to saw her off after I took some Yankee buckshot in Manassas."

O'Grady downed the entire bottle—which Castleberry had also taken the liberty of doctoring—belched, and smacked his lips. He nodded and said, "Not bad. Not bad at all. In fact—"

O'Grady stuck out his bum leg and kicked at the air with it. "I'll be damned," he said excitedly. "I swear I can feel some blood circulatin' agin . . ." His eyes widened. "My leg's gettin' warmer, swear to Jesus." He looked at the crowd, forty-five pairs of eyes, eager faces, and mouths wide enough to swallow the biggest of hooks. All that was left was for him to reel them in.

"My toes!" O'Grady bellowed. "I can move my toes!"

He tossed the crutch aside and plopped to his butt on the dusty street, yanking his left boot off. Two toes were sticking through a worn-out sock. He wiggled them, and stared in amazement like a year-old baby discovering his feet for the first time. "Well Christ on a crutch . . . look at that. Look at that! Ain't moved them toes in near twenty years."

"In three days," Castleberry said, "you'll be walking proud and erect like the Lord intended men to walk, not all stove-up like the Barbary apes." Castleberry's cold eyes twinkled.

O'Grady reached into his pocket and pulled out some bills. "Gimme six bottles," he said.

"I'll take a bottle too," said a well-dressed man, stepping forward with a sweaty silver dollar clenched in his fist.

"Give me three, please," said Emma Watson, the parson's wife.

Emma was the deciding factor. In a matter of seconds, Castleberry was deluged with outstretched hands offering money. People bought three and four bottles at a time, clamoring to partake of Castleberry's brew.

Fortunately, the supply met the demand until, barely ten minutes and hundreds of dollars later, Castleberry held out the last bottle to Jug Jackson.

"For you, dear sir," Castleberry said. "On the house."

"Ah, what the hell," Jug said, taking it. "Couldn't hurt."

The thing Slocum hated the most about coming to after being unconscious was that a body never felt refreshed, like after a good nap or a solid forty winks. A man's body was still hungry for rest; being unconscious didn't rejuvenate a man the way sleep did.

Still, during the last hour or so, sleep did come, if only fleetingly. Slocum was dreaming of Midnight Rose. They were making passionate love, and Midnight Rose was planting wet, juicy kisses all over his face. Slocum, in his dream, wanted more, and opened his mouth and gave Midnight Rose the tongue. She returned it, French-kissing him deeply.

Immediately he knew something was wrong. Even in a dream, he knew that Midnight Rose didn't have hair on her face. He swam back to consciousness and forced his eyes open. His horse was licking his face, nudging him from time to time with her cold nose.

"Good girl," he said weakly.

And then came the pain.

His entire lower body felt on fire, excruciating waves that slammed like a hundred sledgehammers through his back. He tried to raise his head and dizziness washed over him. He'd lost a lot of blood.

Getting up and onto his horse, Slocum knew, would be a

new adventure in agony, but it had to be done if he wanted
to live. Slocum vaguely remembered being bushwhacked
and dumped down a ravine. He'd had the good fortune
of rolling to a stop at the base of a fir tree. He grabbed
its bark and painfully hoisted himself to his feet, hugging
the fir like a long-lost lover. The chestnut stood patiently
next to him; now came the really hard part. He slid a foot
into a stirrup, fighting back the luxury of fainting. He
somehow managed to mount his horse. His spurs hit the
horse's flanks and he took up the reins holding a saddle
horn with one hand for support. Despite the fact that he
was very close to death, he was still extremely angry. Not
only had he been shot, but somewhere along the line he
had lost his hat and was in no condition to look for it.

Now there would really be hell to pay.

6

Even though he was hanging on to consciousness by the most slender of threads, Slocum heard the fiddle and washboard music half a mile from town.

He didn't recall any square dance scheduled for that evening. Hell, it was only a Thursday, but from the sounds of it, a celebration of some sort was in full swing. In his weakened condition, he never made the connection between the snake oil bastard who'd ambushed him and what sounded like a wild party in Brushwood Gulch.

He wanted to spur his horse into a gallop but knew he wasn't capable of withstanding the additional pain. As it was, he felt like keeling over into the trail dust. Only his belt, strapped around both the saddlehorn and his wrist, kept him from falling onto his face.

Twenty minutes later, Slocum rode into the middle of Main Street. Sure enough, a good portion of the townsfolk were whooping it up, dancing wildly and drinking from bottles that looked suspiciously like those peddled by Dr. Castleberry and his merry band of cutthroats.

The party, from the looks of things, was winding down. The fiddling came in fits and starts and a dozen or so people were lying in the muddy street, empty bottles of elixir beside them. The town sawbones, Doc Lockhart, was rushing busily from one prone figure to another. Midnight Rose was assisting him, as were her girls. Those that weren't out cold or in a worse condition were puking their guts out.

Slocum, feeling the very last of his strength ebbing away, managed to pull out his gun and fire two shots into the air. Not surprisingly, he was ignored; he guessed that a thousand shots had been fired into the air that evening, judging from the scores of empty shells that littered the ground.

"I'm gettin' too old for this shit," Slocum muttered, giving up the ghost. He loosened the belt from the saddlehorn and toppled off his horse.

"I think he's coming around."

Slocum recognized the voice; it belonged to Midnight Rose. What a lovely sight to open one's eyes to, if only he were able. Finally, he managed to force them open to see the pretty but worried face of his beloved staring down at him.

"He's awake, Doctor," she said, a small smile crossing her lips.

Doc Lockhart suddenly loomed large over Slocum.

"How do you feel, Slocum?" he asked as Midnight Rose wiped his face with a cool towel.

"Don't ask," he said, his throat drier than a creekbed after a drought. "How long have I been out?"

"Nearly two days," Midnight Rose informed him. "But don't worry. Doc got the bullet out and there's no infection."

They were in Midnight Rose's room. Slocum immediately recognized the aroma of the sweetly scented silk sheets.

"I'm obliged to you, Doc," Slocum rasped. "Would it be possible to get a drink of water?"

Midnight Rose brought the glass to his lips and tipped it. The cold water slid down his parched throat like cool velvet.

"You're a lucky man, Slocum," Doc Lockhart said. "Another hour and we'd have been singing psalms over you."

"Castleberry," Slocum said. "Son of a bitch back shot me."

"He also poisoned half the town," Lockhart said, checking Slocum's heartbeat with a stethoscope. "Killed four people and permanently blinded six more with that rotgut he was peddling. If I hadn't been out at the Archer place deliverin' Maudie's third daughter . . ."

"Where's Jug?" Slocum asked.

"He was the first to go," Midnight Rose said.

"Camphor, benzene, chloral hydrate, laudanum, malt residue, a touch of morphine, and enough denatured alcohol to kill a healthy moose," Lockhart said disgustedly. "Burned a hole right through his belly. *Told* the old fool he was one drink away from the great hereafter."

"Where were you?" Slocum asked Midnight Rose with as much anger as he could muster.

She bristled. "Running my business," she snapped. "If you'd done your job the way you were supposed to—"

"Leave him be, Rose," Lockhart said, checking Slocum's bandages. "He's too weak to fight back."

"Like hell," she said.

"Which way did they go?" Slocum asked.

"We're not sure," Midnight Rose said. "Henry Harper

and some of the others wanted to form a posse, but a whole day had passed and—"

"Wire Will Price, the marshal in Denver," Slocum said, feeling light-headed, knowing he was about to pass out again. "Odds are Castleberry's headed his way."

Slocum blacked out, and it was nearly another day before he opened his eyes again.

"Come on, eat," Midnight Rose snapped, forcing the hot golden liquid down Slocum's throat.

He'd been conscious for a solid six hours now and was feeling a little stronger, though guilty for laying flat on his back when he should have been tracking down Jug's killers. Midnight Rose had dutifully wired Marshal Price in Denver, who'd wired back that a man matching Castleberry's description—accompanied by two sinister-looking types—had boarded a train heading east to Chicago. They'd sold their horses to a local stable, while their wagon had been set on fire and was found smoldering a mile outside town.

Midnight Rose dipped the empty spoon back into the soup. Slocum saw two white balls, the size of large walnuts, floating in a sea of murky, yellow broth.

"What are those white things?" Slocum asked. "Look like pale prairie oysters."

"They're called *matzoh* balls," Midnight Rose said. "They're good for you."

She cut one up and fed it to him. It tasted pretty good. They were just light enough as solid food not to come right back up his throat again. Slocum devoured the soup greedily.

"What'd you call those things again?" Slocum asked, feeding himself now, scarfing up the last of the tasty dumplings.

"*Matzoh* balls," Midnight Rose said. "A Jewish delicacy. Made with unleavened bread. Where I come from, we let them harden for a week and use them as weapons."

Slocum burped heartily. "I don't doubt it," he said. "Don't suppose anyone here in town had the brains to wire the depot in Chicago to find out which way Castleberry was headed."

"You're not the only one who knows how to think, Slocum," Midnight Rose said, somewhat sarcastically. "I'm waiting on a reply to my telegram to the stationmaster there."

"You're pretty clever for a Yankee," Slocum said, smiling.

Norman Jones, the idiot son of the widow Jones, rushed excitedly into the room, followed by the rotund Virginia, the Negro maid.

"It's here, it's here!" Norman cried, the spittle on his lips making him look like a mad dog. "The telegram from Chicago. Is that near Paris?"

"I'ze sorry, Miz Rose," Virginia said. "I tried to keep him downstairs, but—"

"It's okay, Virginia," Midnight Rose said, snatching the telegram from Norman's hand. "Just get him out of here."

Virginia ushered Norman out of the room as Midnight Rose unfolded the telegram. She read, " 'PER YOUR WIRE 9/23, MEN MATCHING DESCRIPTION SEEN BOARDING 8 P.M. TRAIN TO NYC'S GRAND CENTRAL ON EVE OF 9/25 STOP IDENTIFIED BY PINKERTON HORACE JONES AS SAMUEL STEPPE OF NYC STOP ALIASES WEST SIDE SAMMY, SLATS MCCOY, AND JEDADIAH EUSTACE CASTLEBERRY STOP WANTED FOR AN ASSORTMENT OF FELONIES RANGING FROM EMBEZZLE-

MENT TO 2ND DEGREE MURDER, FROM ST. LOU-
IS TO BALTIMORE STOP REPORTED BASED IN
NEW YORK'S HELL'S KITCHEN AREA STOP CON-
SIDERED EXTREMELY DANGEROUS STOP PRO-
CEED WITH CAUTION STOP SIGNED, GERALD
T. BLANEY, STATIONMASTER, UNION STATION
CHICAGO STOP.'"

Slocum reached over from his sickbed and snatched the
telegram from Midnight Rose. He read it for himself, to
digest the information firsthand.

"Hell's Kitchen," he murmured. "Never been to hell
myself. You're from New York. What's it like?"

"It's a nice place if you're in the mood to die," she
said. "What'd you have in mind?"

"I'm going to bring him back and watch him hang,"
Slocum said.

"The hell you are," Midnight Rose said. "Doc Lockhart
said you're not completely healed yet. He said—"

"Doc's never walked around in my boots," Slocum said,
swinging his legs out of the bed. Doc Lockhart was right;
it hurt like hell.

Slocum had some healing to do. He also had a job to
do. Castleberry, or Steppe, or whatever his name was,
had shot him in the back and had killed his deputy, Jug
Jackson. If that wasn't bad enough, four others in Brushwood Gulch had died by his hand. Slocum's conscience—
not to mention his pride—would not let their deaths go
unavenged, especially Jug's.

"Gimme my pants," he groaned, pain shooting up his
limbs as he reached for his holster, which was hanging
around the bedpost. The sudden movement caused the
color to drain from Slocum's face. He felt faint again.
He fought the dizziness and let it pass. He put his pants
on and was sliding into his boots when Midnight Rose

tried to ease him back onto the bed.

"You just lay there and rest," she scolded. "You're weaker than a newborn calf, John Slocum, and in no shape to—"

Slocum brushed her away and leaped from the bed, looking for his shirt. "Shut your trap, Rose," he said, "and help me get dressed. I got to get to New York."

"Slocum," she said, "you don't understand. If you put the Barbary Coast and New Orleans both into the middle of hell, it would still be a Sunday school picnic compared to what you're going to find in New York. From the Bowery to Harlem, are a million people. Half of them will shoot you in the back, and the other half will take your money while you're lying there bleeding to death."

"No," Slocum said, buttoning his shirt. "You don't understand. Every man's got a code of justice he lives by, and if he stops living it, he ain't no man."

"Code, schmode," Midnight Rose pooh-poohed with a wave of her hand. "It's a different world, Slocum, and this one-man posse thing won't cut the mustard in that town. Every rat—the kind on two legs—can always find a hole to hide in. You're one man, Slocum, not an army, and you'd need a hundred regiments just to cover the Bowery alone. You're not just gunning for a couple of Kreeg brothers now, Slocum. New York is the big time. They don't play by the same rules you do."

"Save your breath, Rosie," Slocum said. His expression was grim; his jaw clenched tightly, his face rigid with determination despite the pain as he strapped on his holster.

Seeing that her words were not having the desired effect, Midnight Rose tried a different approach.

"Let me put it to you another way," she said, throwing her arms around him. She held him tightly, whispering in his ear, "You go Slocum, and you'll never get out of there alive." She kissed him deeply, then added, "There's no future in loving a dead man."

Slocum broke away from her and sat down on the bed. He patted the spot next to him and said, "Sit."

Rose sat.

"Rosie," he said. "You hired me to protect the people of this town and I failed. Some good folks are six feet under. You may be right; I may never come back, but if I don't at least try, then I've betrayed this badge and everything it stands for."

He stood and walked to the door—and immediately felt light-headed and grabbed a coatrack for support.

"Great," Midnight Rose said. "You want to go two thousand miles and you can't even walk five feet."

"I'm fine," Slocum said stubbornly, though he felt anything but.

"I don't suppose you've given any thought to what we're supposed to use for a lawman while you're gone," Rose said.

"Wire the federal marshal in Denver," Slocum said. "They'll send a deputy marshal out to keep an eye on things. Mention my name."

"One last question," Midnight Rose said. "What were you planning to use for money?"

"I was hoping to get an advance on my salary," he said.

"Do you know what *chutzpah* is, Slocum?" she said indignantly. "You're on the job just over a week, been on your back for three days, and you're asking for money?"

"I'll get it somewhere else if I have to," Slocum said, sinking into a chair.

Midnight Rose went to the bureau and opened the top drawer. She rummaged around and pulled out a silk purse.

"There's two hundred dollars in here, Slocum, and it's all yours if you promise to wait twenty-four hours when you'll be stronger."

"Deal," Slocum said without hesitation, too weak to bargain with her and knowing the futility of even trying.

"Sheriff Slocum," Mayor Everett said. "Is this trip really necessary?"

Slocum watched as Norman Jones, the widow Jones' idiot son, saddled up his horse. Everett had been pleading with Slocum for the better part of an hour to reconsider his foolhardy quest into the "bowels of evil" as Everett referred to New York.

"I mean, after all, Slocum," Everett continued. "This impulsive, reckless mission of yours is doomed to fail, and with you being too weak to even pursue a stray calf, much less . . ."

"Don't bother, Horton," Midnight Rose said to the mayor. "I've been giving him the same argument for two days. He doesn't listen to anyone but himself." She dabbed her eyes with a handkerchief.

Bubba Chin, the proprietor of the chop suey emporium, came scurrying up to the assembled crowd—Midnight Rose, Mayor Everett, all of Rose's staff, and a dozen or so townspeople who'd come to see their sheriff off. Though a second-generation Chinese-American, Bubba still dressed like his ancestors: sandals, white socks, a floppy straw hat and a black robe. He was toting a wicker basket. The appetizing aroma of chow mein and pepper steak almost overpowered the whores' cheap French perfume and the fresher horse patties on the street.

"For your long trip," Bubba Chin offered with a smile, handing the basket to Slocum.

"Smells good, Bubba," Slocum said. "But I'm afraid I

won't have room in my saddlebags to carry it. Besides,"
he added, lifting the white towel covering the food and
taking a whiff—the Chinese food smelled delightful— "it's
only a four-hour ride to Denver."

"Eat on train," Bubba said.

Slocum shook his head. "Keep it warm for me, Bubba.
I'll be back."

"You blave man, Slocum."

"She's all ready, Sheriff," Norman Jones announced,
slapping the chestnut's flank.

The horse responded on cue and galloped riderless off
down Main Street. The entire crowd turned to watch. The
truth gradually dawned on the dim-witted Norman, who
ran off in pursuit.

Slocum turned to Midnight Rose. As he gazed into her
big blue eyes, he knew his feelings for her would still be
there when he got back and then some. The sensation was
akin to heartburn or maybe squatting on a cactus for a day,
but this pain actually felt pretty good. *Could this be love?*
Slocum wondered. He was a little rusty on that particular
feeling.

She was in his arms before he could blink.

"You take care of yourself, Slocum," she said. It came
out as a hoarse whisper. "And never eat the trout on the
train."

"Why not?" he asked, gazing into her eyes and wanting
to dive deeply into them.

"Never eat fish when you don't know if it's fresh," she
said, knowing she was crazy for this *meshugah* prairie
tramp.

"How about the chicken?" Slocum asked, wanting only
to slide his tongue down her throat.

"Chicken is fine," she whispered in his ear.

"I hate chicken." Their lips met, perhaps for the last

time. Slocum curled his arms around her, and her body felt good against his—even better, it felt right. The longer he held her close, the tougher it would be to leave, he knew.

"I'd best be going," he said.

Norman had returned with Slocum's horse by this time. Slocum swung into the saddle and grabbed the reins, doing his best to conceal the pain that sliced through his side like a red-hot musket blade.

He reined the chestnut around, pointing her west toward Denver.

"As the mayor of Brushwood Gulch," Everett started, "I must go on record as opposing this foolishness."

"Shut up, Horton," Midnight Rose said. "You got two weeks, Slocum. After that, we look for a new lawman."

"Fair enough," Slocum said. He spurred the horse and they galloped off down Main Street.

Midnight Rose, with moist eyes, watched Slocum disappear into the distance.

She dabbed at her eyes with a lace hanky and turned to Carter Fawcett, who ran the Western Union telegraph office.

"I need to send a telegram, Mr. Fawcett," she said, taking his arm and leading him toward the office.

"Where to, Miss Midnight?" he asked.

"Back east," she said. She turned once more toward the street, where Slocum's dust was slowly settling.

"You'll be back, Slocum," she said softly to herself. "If I have anything to say about it."

7

"Grand Central Station, next and last stop, Grand Central Station, New York City," cried the conductor.

Slocum grunted and smashed out his cheroot in the ashtray under the window. They had the nerve to call this space a stateroom; it was roughly the size of half an outhouse. The bed was too narrow for a decent night's sleep; for one thing, a man had to be a midget if he didn't want his butt sticking out into the cold and his feet pressed against the wall of the compartment. From Denver to Chicago, and then on to New York, a total of five nights, Slocum had slept barely ten hours.

Even worse, in the passenger car when he'd pulled out his whiskey flask, Slocum was told by the officious conductor that drinking was permitted only in the lounge car, and that the consumption of one's own supply was forbidden.

Ultimately, Slocum had spent most of the trip in the lounge car, where a shot ran for seventy-five cents— pretty pricey at that. At that point, he'd stopped drinking and read newspapers. The further east he got, the more stories he read about senseless shootings, stabbings, and various crimes that would put any man's fillings to the test. In Pittsburgh, the train had taken on the New York papers, which Slocum read with horrified fascination. New York made even the most wide open Colorado mining town look like a cakewalk. There were tales of political corruption, lawlessness, riots, murder, and crimes so perverse that Slocum was convinced that the entire population of this city was suffering from rabies.

At the same time though, the evil of this place might prove somewhat attractive, in much the same way Slocum was pulled to the Barbary Coast every couple of years. With danger came a certain form of excitement that caused his blood to flow faster, and nothing helped a gunslinger keep alert than a rush of fast-moving blood now and then.

In anticipation of his arrival, Slocum dressed in his Sunday best: blue jacket, stiffly starched white shirt, bolo tie, and boots free of mud, shined by the Negro porter.

The train lumbered into Grand Central Station, passing decrepit shanty towns on the outskirts of the city, followed by crumbling tenements. Slocum was amazed to see herds of people crowding the narrow cobblestone streets, all moving quickly like their butts were on fire. Buggies, wagons, and streetcars competed with the roiling masses of humanity for space on the streets. Even more amazing were the trains that ran high above the street on wobbly pillars of steel. Everything seemed to be covered in a coat of grime.

The train lurched to a halt, and Slocum gathered up his bags—a battered leather one he bought in Denver—that contained his entire wardrobe: three shirts, a second pair of blue jeans, two pairs of socks with a total of three holes in them, a pair of long johns, and plenty of ammunition.

"Damn," was all Slocum could say as he stepped into the main terminal in Grand Central Station. Slocum had read about the Sistine Chapel, and judging from the distance between the top of his head and the roof of Grand Central, the two might have been built by the same man. Murals of the constellations and how they evolved into the ancient Greek gods artfully covered the curved ceiling, leaving Slocum breathless.

Slocum followed the crowds toward a sign that was marked "exit," assuming that they were heading into the streets. Out of the corner of his eye he saw two Negro men—one a midget and the other tall and skinny with only one leg. Slocum's curiosity got the better of him when he heard harmonica music coming from the midget. The one-legged Negro was doing a two-step minus one, with the help of a cane, in time to the music. A small crowd was watching them perform. Leaning against a wooden stool was a crudely painted sign that read, "One-Legged Lincoln and His Very Small Minstrel Show." Slocum watched for a couple of minutes, enthralled by the performance. When it abruptly ended, One-Legged Lincoln started passing the hat for contributions. Several in the crowd tossed in pennies and drifted away, leaving Slocum standing there alone, clapping enthusiastically.

"Mighty fancy stepping, son, mighty fancy," Slocum said.

"Thank you, sir," said One-Legged Lincoln, holding out the hat.

"I'm afraid I don't have any change to spare," Slocum said. "But I'm mighty impressed."

He turned to walk away. One-Legged Lincoln managed to hop up and wallop Slocum in the ass with his cane; before he could even react to this, the midget punched him in the crotch, reaching up to do it. Slocum doubled over, dropping his bag. The midget snapped it up and disappeared into the crowd. The bastards had bushwhacked him. Before the pain had subsided, Slocum crouched helplessly and watched One-Legged Lincoln also melt into the teeming mass of humanity that was New York.

A beefy Irish policeman sauntered over, swinging his billy club.

"Might there be a problem, sir?" he asked with an Irish brogue thick enough to slice with a hatchet.

"I think I've just been robbed," Slocum said, managing to straighten up now. "No money, thank the Lord, but all my clothes . . ."

"Was one of them a one-legged man of color?" asked the cop.

"In fact, I believe he was," Slocum said.

"Was the other a dwarf, also of color?" asked the cop now.

"I think you're catching on," Slocum said.

"That would be One-Legged Lincoln and Little Elmo," the cop said. "Thieves both."

"Do tell," Slocum said. "Any chance of getting my suitcase back?"

The cop twirled his billy club, looking thoughtful. It required some effort. "I wouldn't be thinking so, sir," he said. "Odds are they're halfway uptown by now."

"Fine," Slocum said, pulling out his Colt. "Which way is uptown?"

"You best be puttin' that away, lad," said the cop. "Otherwise I'll have to be haulin' ye in for disturbin' the peace."

"I'm sorry if my getting robbed woke you up," Slocum said, "but I want my goods back."

"Your goods are likely being sold on a street corner about now," said the cop. "My advice to you is to buy some new ones and go about your business."

"The hell you say," Slocum said, pulling his tin star out of his shirt pocket. "I'm a lawman, too, from Colorado, and where I come from, we make an effort to uphold the law and not just when it's convenient."

The cop's face started turning ruddy red as the anger set in. "You'd be wise to watch your mouth, stranger." He jabbed the billy club into Slocum's belly, knocking the wind out of him. Slocum doubled over in pain as the cop turned his back and started to saunter away. "Top of the morning to you, friend."

Slocum recovered quickly and kicked the beefy cop firmly in the backside.

"And a tap in the morning to you, too," Slocum said.

The cop turned, billy club raised and ready to strike. Slocum was prepared. He landed a solid right to the cop's chin, sending the billy club flying, where it struck a man hawking corn on the cob on the back of the head. The cop's head popped back like a cap being snapped off a bottle of sarsaparilla.

A crowd had gathered by this point. One man said to Slocum, "You better make tracks, pal, or else you'll have a dozen more on your tail."

Slocum wisely heeded the stranger's words and made his way quickly toward the station exit. Outside, a line of hansom cabs were waiting for passengers. Slocum hopped into the first one. The driver, a short, cherub-faced Irishman—were there any other kinds of people in New York, Slocum wondered—turned to Slocum with a huge grin. His teeth were the same color as his hair—copper.

"Stumpy Malarkey's the name, sir. Where might you be wantin' to go?" he asked.

"Anywhere," Slocum said. "I just hit a policeman, and I've heard that can be bad for your health."

"Indeed it is, sir," Stumpy agreed, and snapped the reins. The hansom jerked forward across Forty-second Street toward Fifth Avenue. The ride was bumpier than any stagecoach he'd ever ridden over rocky terrain.

Stumpy said to Slocum, over his shoulder, "You got to go somewhere, sir. Might you be wantin' some feminine companionship?"

"No," Slocum said.

"Perhaps you'd prefer a samplin' of the grape then," Stumpy offered. "Stumpy Malarkey knows a saloon on Tenth Avenue where the whiskey is hard and the women are easy."

"Take me to the nearest police precinct," Slocum said.

"Weren't thinking of turning yourself in, were you, mate?" Stumpy asked. "As one who's felt the sting of many a cop's slapstick, I wouldn't be recommending it."

"I'll take my chances," Slocum said.

"It's your hide, cowboy," Stumpy replied with a shrug, and snapped his whip. "Make haste, horsey."

The horse broke into a trot, and ten minutes later they pulled up in front of a depressingly dark gray stone building on West Forty-Seventh Street that reminded Slocum of a penitentiary in Kansas he'd seen once.

"Tenth Precinct, sir," Stumpy announced.

Slocum reached into his pocket. "How much do I owe you?"

"This one's on the house," Stumpy told him. "Me gut's tellin' me you'll be needin' every cent for bail money."

Slocum was impressed. Contrary to what he'd been told, not every New Yorker was lower than a snake's toes.

"Don't be so sure." Slocum handed Stumpy a ten-dollar bill. "I won't be here long. Wait for me."

"Whatever you say, sir," Stumpy said, taking the money.

"And be here when I get back."

"You can trust Stumpy Malarkey, yes sir," he chirped.

Slocum strode through the heavy wooden doors of the precinct. The place was a beehive of activity: policemen everywhere, smoking, swearing, booking, and sometimes beating suspects. Had it not been for the blue uniforms, he wouldn't have been able to tell one from the other.

Cracked and yellowed wanted posters dotted the walls. The criminals, all locals, had names like Hammerhead Garrity, Barney Beans, Terrible Tommy Sullivan, Piker Edwards, and Baby-Eater Babcock. Slocum had run up against some pretty bad desperados, but none of them could compare to the gallery of pug-uglies on display here.

Slocum walked up to the booking desk. A bored-looking cop sat behind it, an open copy of the *Police Gazette* perched on his wide expanse of girth. Cigar smoke billowed up from behind the newspaper.

"Pardon me," Slocum said.

A red, fleshy face peered over the top of the *Gazette*. He looked a lot like the cop Slocum had cold-cocked in Grand Central Station.

"Yeah?" the desk sergeant asked. He sounded like a hoarse bullfrog.

"I need some information," Slocum said.

The corpulent cop eyed Slocum suspiciously. "Go to church every Sunday, stay away from the bottle, resist the temptations of the flesh, and you'll get into Heaven," he remarked.

He returned to his newspaper.

"Jesus Christ," Slocum muttered, and struck a match on the side of the desk. He lit the bottom of the paper and within seconds it was aflame, though it took the dense

desk sergeant two thirds of the page to realize his paper
was on fire.

"Sweet Jesus, mother of Mary!" he cried, jumping up
and dropping the paper to the floor, where he stomped on
it. He looked at Slocum, who was casually shaking out the
match. He reached up and grabbed the sergeant's necktie,
yanking the fat man belly-first across the desk.

"Are you going to help me or do I have to burn this
entire Sodom of a city to the ground?" Slocum asked
through gritted teeth.

Before the sergeant could even reply, Slocum felt a
thousand hands grabbing his arms, his sides, and even his
ears. Half a dozen cops tried to drag him away. Slocum
held firm to the sergeant's necktie, dragging the fat man
across his desk in the process. Billy clubs painfully slapped
Slocum's hands and the backs of his knees. He summoned
every last ounce of his strength and managed to break free
of the six policemen. One to his immediate left was on
him in a second, billy club swinging. Slocum ducked and
his hat flew across the room. Slocum was up faster than a
scared armadillo, planting a hefty haymaker on the cop's
nose. Slocum felt bone disintegrate and blood gush onto
his fist.

At the same time, he felt a pointy boot connect with his
kidneys and two billy clubs smashed against the back of his
neck and the small of his back, paralyzing him temporarily.
These Irish cops, he thought dimly, were pretty tough.

But I'm tougher, Slocum said to himself and shook off
the pain for the time being. He elbowed a second cop in
the breadbasket and jammed his left spur into the meaty
calf of a third.

This amazing spectacle—the tall, lanky cowboy taking
on six burly Irish policemen—caused all activity to cease
in the station house. Cop and criminal alike stopped to

watch, both impressed by Slocum's tenacity.

A door to one of the private offices swung open. Stenciled on the glass was "Kevin Flannery, Chief of Detectives." Flannery stepped out to see what the ruckus was about. He was a small man—five foot seven at the most—but every inch was street tough. His features resembled a rock chiseled by the effects of hard times.

He folded his arms across his chest and watched with some amusement as this resilient cowboy took on a good portion of the Tenth Precinct.

Slocum, meanwhile, continued waging his war against New York's finest—and was doing a pretty good job of making them look like New York's worst. One cop tried to pin Slocum's arms behind his back, while another delivered a series of hard blows to Slocum's belly. Slocum kicked the puncher in the groin and broke free of the cop holding him. He spun on his heels and slammed his fist into the cop's left eye.

By this time, a good portion of the cops had descended upon Slocum again, having shaken the cobwebs out of their skulls. They wrestled him to the floor and began punching every inch of his body. Slocum squirmed and kicked and clawed, but it didn't look good. He was definitely outnumbered and out-fisted and knew it, but he'd be damned if he wouldn't go out gracefully.

"That'll teach you to trifle with me," the desk sergeant bellowed, rubbing his sore nose.

They continued to pummel Slocum mercilessly from every direction. Nobody but Flannery noticed the tin star fall from Slocum's pocket to the floor.

"To hell with you!" Slocum cried out amidst the flurry of fists. "All I wanted was a little help and you treat me like I'm a housefly."

"You're no better than a housefly," the desk sergeant cried. "Finish him off, boys," he told the six cops, who continued punching and kicking Slocum.

He was nearly unconscious when he heard a shot fired into the air. He dimly saw chunks of plaster and dust fall to the floor. The beating stopped as if by magic.

"Hold it right there," Detective Kevin Flannery yelled. "Leave him be."

The punches and kicks stopped, but the cops still held him firmly.

"What the hell's going on here?" Flannery asked.

"The man was disrespectful," the desk sergeant whined. "Set me paper on fire, he did."

"About time someone did," Flannery commented. He motioned to the six cops. "Get him to his feet."

They roughly dragged Slocum up off the floor and onto his feet. Blood was trickling from his nose and mouth. Flannery walked over and picked up Slocum's tin star.

"This belong to you?" he asked.

"John Slocum," he said. "Sheriff of Brushwood Gulch, Colorado."

"What brings you to New York, Slocum?"

"A citizen of your fair city killed some people in my town," Slocum said, wiping the blood from his mouth with the back of his wrist.

"And who might that be?" Flannery wanted to know.

"Goes by the name of Jedadiah Castleberry," Slocum said.

Flannery's eyebrows arched upward. "Castleberry did you say?"

"You know him?" Slocum asked.

"Let him go," Flannery told the cops. They released Slocum, who struggled to stand erect without wobbling. As of today he'd officially had his ass kicked from sea to shining sea, but damned if he'd give these blue-suited bastards the satisfaction of knowing it.

"But Mr. Flannery," the desk sergeant protested. "The man resisted arrest and battered officers of the law! Thirty days in the jug will cool him off."

"Thirty days'll just make him madder," Flannery said. He walked over and took Slocum's arm. "You a drinking man, Sheriff?"

"I've been known to toss back a few," Slocum replied.

"Let's step into my office," Flannery said, leading Slocum toward it.

"But sir," the desk sergeant said, "the man is a criminal."

"Have you been promoted to judge, Sergeant O'Rourke?" Flannery asked.

"No sir, but—"

"In the future, O'Rourke," Flannery said, "try to remember that you're a public servant and not a private asshole."

Flannery poured Slocum another drink.

" . . . And that's when the Kreeg brothers made their way over to Colorado," Slocum said, and took a swallow. "I'd been tracking them for weeks."

Flannery was fascinated by Slocum's exploits of the West. He'd read a number of dime novels and newspaper accounts on the subject and had always written the stories off to overworked imaginations. But here was John Slocum, a flesh-and-blood example of frontier America, confirming nearly every wild yarn Flannery had ever read.

"Tell me more about Castleberry," Flannery said.

"I told you everything," Slocum said, downing the last of the smooth Scotch and slamming the glass on Flannery's desk. "Tell me where I can find him."

"I don't know, exactly," Flannery said. He walked over to the door and opened it. "O'Rourke," he shouted. "Bring me the file on the Hudson Dusters gang." He turned to Slocum and said, "I'm pretty sure I know your man."

O'Rourke appeared at the door, file in hand. He glared at Slocum, his eyes showing the anger and frustration he felt.

"Thank you, Sergeant," Flannery said, slamming the door in his face. Flannery leafed through the folder. "Just as I thought. Jed Castleberry, real name Samuel Steppe."

"I know," Slocum said. "The Pinkertons told me."

"Oh, yes," Flannery remembered, almost fondly. "A member of Razor Riley's waterfront gang." He read some more. "Looks like Sammy's come a long way since we last met. You say he poisoned some people in Colorado?"

"That's correct," Slocum said.

"Interesting. Didn't know Steppe was working the snake oil circuit out West, though I'm not surprised. A lot of our bad city boys head for greener pastures when things get too hot here. Steppe's got a record longer than the Bowery," Flannery remarked, leafing through the file. "We butted heads when I was walking a beat on the West Side six years ago. Shaking the storekeepers down for protection, if I remember correctly." Flannery looked at Slocum, remembering. "Smarter than most of the hoodlums in Hell's Kitchen. More educated. Had a line of blarney smoother than twelve-year-old Scotch. Destined for better things, no doubt about it."

"I'll be sleeping poorly 'til I get him," Slocum said.

"Even if he is here, Slocum," Flannery said, "you'd have better luck finding a needle in a haystack. This is New York, not the cornfields of Kansas."

"I'm from Colorado, not Kansas," Slocum said. "Mind if I skim your files?"

"Help yourself," Flannery said, handing it over.

Slocum leafed through Castleberry/Steppe's thick dossier. He didn't care about the bastard's other crimes, he only wanted to hang the man for those committed in his town.

"Who's this Razor Riley?" Slocum asked.

"A murdering scalawag who'd slice open a man's throat for the pennies in his pocket," Flannery said, rummaging now through a battered metal filing cabinet. He pulled out a fuzzy photograph and handed it to Slocum. He'd run up against some pretty mean-looking hombres before, but the face in the photo made him gasp audibly.

"That's Razor Riley," Flannery said.

"It certainly is," Slocum said, his voice barely above a whisper.

"He's the leader of the Hudson Dusters, a gang of thieves and cutthroats who make their headquarters down at Magpie Maggie's saloon on the West Side piers—the very seat of scum and villainy this side of hell itself," Flannery said, lighting his pipe.

No doubt about it, Razor Riley was one mean desperado. Even though the photo was fuzzy, Slocum could see the ugly, jagged knife scar that ran down Riley's left cheek. The right side of his nose was a gaping hole. "Had most of his nose bit off in a fight," Flannery told him. What was left of his nose had been considerably flattened. A battered derby was perched atop Riley's square head; a few unruly strands of hair covered his forehead. His mouth was a thin, bloodless slit and his right ear was also partially gone; Slocum didn't care to learn how. Riley was even uglier than Tomahawk-Face, a blood-thirsty Comanche war chief he'd run up against years earlier.

"You'd best head back home, Slocum," Flannery said. He poured his guest another healthy slug from the bottle. "Even if you managed to find Steppe—and you'll probably get yourself killed long before—and you brought him in, he'd be a free man within six hours. Steppe's tied in with Riley, and Riley's tied in with the devils in Tammany Hall—that's the political machine that runs this city and controls everything, including the police. If it were up to me, Riley and his ilk would be sitting on the bottom of the East River with railroad ties rammed up their buttholes. But I can only do so much."

"A true peace officer doesn't always take the law at face value," Slocum said. "Sometimes we bend 'em a bit, to meet the situation."

"Frontier justice is something we won't tolerate here, John Slocum," Flannery said. "Go outside the law and you're one step away from vigilante rule. Saw enough of it here after the war ended."

"I didn't come here to argue the finer points of the law, Flannery," Slocum said, rising. "I'd be obliged if you told me where I can find this Magpie Maggie's saloon."

"They'll cut a hole in your gullet and rip your tongue out through it, and work their way down until you're gutted like a hog," Flannery warned. "Go back to Colorado, bury your dead, and put Samuel Steppe behind you. You'll live a lot longer."

"Appreciate your concern," Slocum said, and suddenly felt tired all over. He meant well, but men like Flannery—Easterners in general—could never tell the difference between the written laws of man and those unwritten by the Almighty. They could figure out the man, but never his soul. It was a lot like his Aunt Amelia used to say: "Never try to teach a pig to sing. It wastes your time and annoys the hell out of the pig."

"Thing is, it's something I got to do," Slocum said.

"A week in the hoosegow might change your mind," Flannery said. "For your own protection, of course." He kind of liked John Slocum, especially what he stood for. Flannery had traded lead at Gettysburg with many like Slocum, and even though they'd been the enemy, Flannery had admired their tenacity and willingness to die for the South.

"That's your choice, Slocum," he added. "Go back to Colorado or cool your heels in jail."

"Jail?"

"I couldn't in all good conscience allow you to venture out into my city and get yourself dead," Flannery said.

"Okay," Slocum said, sounding resigned. "I guess you're right. It's too much for one man alone." He turned to leave, then stuck out his hand. "I appreciate your help, Flannery."

Flannery grasped Slocum's hand. "You're doing the right thing, Slocum. Couldn't let a fellow peace offic-er—"

With his right hand shaking Flannery's, Slocum lashed out with his left fist and connected with Flannery's eye. Slocum released his grip and Flannery sailed back and slammed into the wall, the back of his head kissing it passionately. He slithered down dazed, his eyes crossed.

Slocum turned on his heels and was slamming the door behind him even before Flannery's butt hit the floor. He strode through the busy precinct with a polite smile on his face, praying Stumpy hadn't taken off with his money.

Slocum's luck was definitely holding. Stumpy and his cab hadn't moved an inch from where he'd left them. Slocum sprinted down the steps and then vaulted into the buggy. Stumpy snapped the reins and off they went.

"Where to, my new friend?" Stumpy asked as they bounced over the cobblestone street.

"Magpie Maggie's saloon," Slocum said.

Stumpy jerked the reins, bringing the horse to an abrupt halt and flinging Slocum forward in his seat. Stumpy turned to him, wide-eyed and pale.

"Was that Magpie Maggie's you said, sir?" Stumpy asked.

"On the West Side piers," Slocum said. "Do you know where to find it?"

"If only I didn't, sir," Stumpy said, his hand clutching his throat. "A deadly place, not fit for man nor beast. If it's spirits you're seeking, there are better places—"

Slocum peeled two bills off his rapidly diminishing bankroll. "Twenty dollars if you take me there."

"There ain't enough money in the whole of the world for Stumpy Malarkey to journey into the bowels of hell, no sir."

"Thirty," Slocum said.

"You're not understanding me, sir," Stumpy said. "The waterfront is not on the list of scheduled stops."

Slocum gave Stumpy fifty dollars.

"Get going," Slocum said.

"They say every man has his price," Stumpy said, "and that may be true, but my life is worth more than fifty dollars. I'll not be taking Jesus Christ himself to the waterfront."

"How about sixty?" Slocum asked.

"I'll drop you ten blocks from there," Stumpy offered. "That's as close as I'll be going. Is that agreed?"

"I've come ten states, Stumpy," Slocum said. "Ten blocks won't keep me from what has to be done."

"I'll say a prayer or two for ye soul," Stumpy said, and cracked his whip at the horse. "Downtown, horsey."

8

Even the moon was afraid to be seen in this neighborhood, Slocum thought as Stumpy tooled the buggy down the dark, deserted streets of lower Manhattan. The ugly structures on either side of them loomed up like the gates of purgatory. The screams of men and women alike, shattering windows, and echoing gunshots permeated the night. Blood-splattered meathooks lined the undersides of the packing plant awnings along West Street. Darkened shadows hunched in corners, darting furtively from doorway to doorway. Packs of snarling mad dogs and hundreds of repellent black rats swarmed like a plague across the narrow side streets and alleyways, which were choked with rotting garbage and horseshit.

Crumbling tenements stood side by side, seemingly held together with cheap glue and inhabited by thousands of wretched souls. Puffy-faced women leaned on windowsills covered with pillows. Even at a distance Slocum could tell that their eyes had seen a million horrors and would not be especially shocked at a million more. Children—some barely old enough to walk—were dressed in rags. They congregated in the streets, swinging the carcasses of dead cats and fighting.

Stumpy suddenly brought the buggy to a stop. "This is as far as I'll be going."

"Which way to Magpie Maggie's?" Slocum asked.

"Can't say as I'm sure exactly," Stumpy said, "but ye ain't far." He pointed to a crudely painted sign that read "The Greasy Slide."

"The Slide's one of the safer saloons in this part of town," Stumpy told him. "Someone in there will know where to find Magpie Maggie's."

"Why is it so safe?" Slocum asked.

"I believe you'll find out, sir," Stumpy said. "A man as handsome as yourself won't have any problems getting his questions answered."

"I'll trust your judgment," Slocum said, climbing from the buggy. "I suppose it's pointless to ask you to wait."

Stumpy rode off. Slocum adjusted his hat, hitched up his pants, and strode across the street toward the Greasy Slide. He could see dim lantern light in the tiny window that faced the street; behind it lurched shadows that were definite indications of life, albeit, Slocum guessed, the lowest form possible.

The heavy wooden door was bolted shut from the inside. Slocum pounded on it with his fist until a slit opened up to reveal a thin slice of smoky light. A pair of mean-looking eyes appeared in the slit.

"State your business," growled a man's voice from behind the door.

"Stumpy Malarkey sent me," Slocum said.

"Don't know him and don't want to," said the voice, as raspy as wood against sandpaper.

"He knows you," Slocum said.

"Who do you favor, then?" the voice asked. "State your pleasure."

"I'll take what comes," Slocum responded, not having the slightest inkling as to what this voice was talking about.

The eyes behind the slit were unwavering. "You'll have to do better than that," the voice croaked.

"I'm looking only for a little affection," Slocum said, convinced he was at the doorstep of a whorehouse. "And I've got the money to prove it." Slocum waved his small wad across the slit in the door.

The slit disappeared; Slocum heard muffled male voices behind it. A moment later the heavy wooden door creaked open and a chubby face peered out and scrutinized Slocum. A second face, younger and paler, loomed up above the first.

"Let him in, Caspar," said the second man with a slight lisp.

The heavy wooden door slowly swung open. The faint yellow shadows from the dim gaslights spilled out into the alleyway. Slocum stepped inside. The strains of a waltz could be heard.

Right off the bat, Slocum knew he was not in just any saloon. This one seemed a lot like the joint he'd stepped inside that rainy night in San Francisco a few years earlier. Half the men in this joint looked to be dandies; he'd never seen so many neatly dressed and shaven men—just a little too neat for Slocum's taste. The dandies were sitting at tables with some rough-looking waterfront types, others were dancing with each other to the accompaniment of a four-piece band, all women. Slocum had never seen women musicians before. To his horror, he realized the women were actually men dressed like women. A sick feeling settled in his belly. The men in this place were what he called "rump riders." Slocum made a mental note to strangle Stumpy with his own tongue the first chance he got.

Still, it was too late to back out now. Just because Slocum personally had no desire to play with something he already had, didn't mean these poofs wouldn't get nasty if he insulted them by bolting out the door.

Instead, he stepped up to the bar. The bartender, who also looked suspect, said, "Yeah?"

"Beer," Slocum said, trying to avoid the stare of a well-dressed, middle-aged man who looked like a banker or a lawyer. The man, Slocum noted with mounting disgust, had pure, shit-eating lust in his eyes, the same look a cowpoke had after three months on a drive.

The bartender placed a beer before Slocum, who reached into his pocket to pay. He never got the chance.

"It's paid for, friend," said the bartender with a wink, tilting his head toward the banker.

Slocum glanced at his benefactor. He grinned at Slocum and licked his lips.

"He's a rich man, friend," said the bartender through his teeth. "And he likes the company of cowboys."

Slocum tossed the beer in the bartender's face and slammed the lowlife's face down hard onto the wet bar. He grabbed the dazed barkeep by the hair and gave him a second helping. Beer and blood ran down the bartender's face.

"You got the wrong idea, friend," Slocum said. "The only thing I ride has four legs, not two. Understand?"

"I don't think you understand, pal," snarled a voice behind him, and a second later Slocum was surrounded by three pug-faced thugs. A fourth stood behind Slocum.

One of them, the toughest looking of the bunch, spoke. Despite his bulldog face and bulging muscles, his voice was higher and more feminine sounding than Slocum's spinster aunt.

"I can't say I care for your manners, Mr. Desperado," he lisped. "After all, if you don't like the company, you should go elsewhere."

Behind him, the fourth thug pinched Slocum's left ass cheek. He also felt the cold metal of a blade against his neck.

"I didn't come in here looking for trouble."

"That's what they all say," said the limp-wristed thug. "But it's trouble they all want."

Something snapped in Slocum's brain. In seven hours in this crazed city he'd been beaten, robbed, and harassed at every opportunity. Enough was enough. He elbowed the man behind him in the gut; at the same time, he landed his left spur into the soft calf of the one to his immediate right. A haymaker from his left fist connected with the belly of the first poof. Two went down while a third hopped around on one leg, blood gushing from his calf. The fourth thug barely had time to react before Slocum planted the toe of his boot squarely and firmly between his legs. He doubled over in pain.

"You faggots listen to me!" Slocum cried in an angry rage that brought a shocked hush to the saloon. "I came three thousand miles on a crowded, smelly train, I had my goods stolen and had to fight my way through a hundred of your goddamn police. I took a bullet in my back, I ain't eaten in nine hours, I ain't moved my bowels in three days, and I'm gettin' real tired of the bullshit New York City has to offer. Somebody better give me some goddamned answers or I'll be forced to kick the living daylights out of everyone in this establishment!"

A wiry little man sashayed up to Slocum, love in his eyes.

"How can we help you, handsome?" asked the little dumpling.

"Where can I find Magpie Maggie's saloon?"

"You don't want to go there," the dumpling said. "It's a bad place full of very bad people."

Slocum grabbed the dumpling and slammed him against the wall. "I asked you a question, Mary."

"We do like to play rough, don't we?" the swishy man said, and Slocum realized that the guy was actually enjoying it. "Maybe I'll tell you and maybe I won't."

Slocum grabbed the man's sweetmeats and gave them a very healthy squeeze. The dumpling howled in pain but said, "Two blocks down, on West Street, number forty-one."

"I'm obliged," Slocum said, and released the man's testicles. He turned and walked out the door.

"Aren't you going to hit me?" the little man asked, and damned if he didn't sound disappointed.

Forty-one West Street was a decrepit waterfront shithole made even worse by the stench of the filthy Hudson River. Slocum crossed the cobblestoned street and headed straight for it. The docks were shrouded now in a thick fog, making the place look that much more sinister. Even without the fog, though, moonlight could never penetrate the crumbling tall buildings in this part of town. Slocum cold hear the waves slapping against the rotting pilings. Platoons of fat, black rats scurried boldly past Slocum, giving him no more than a passing glance. In front of the saloon, a couple of drunken sailors were going at it with broken bottles, and they were both scoring lots of points. One sailor was bleeding heavily from a gash in his cheek; the other had red zig-zagging slices across his forehead and nose. Ten feet away, three gorillas in men's clothes were pummeling an old rummy who tried vainly to fend them off with his crutch. Slocum's first reaction was to help the broken-down boozer, but common sense prevailed, and he decided it was probably better not to get involved.

Some insane evangelist standing on a soapbox on the corner ranted on about the bowels of hell and sin and damnation. Even in the foggy distance, Slocum could see the red madness in the preacher's eyes. Passersby gleefully took turns heaving rotten fruit and bottles at him, but his maniacal monologue continued uninterrupted. Slocum agreed with the preacher on one point: this city, he decided, was as close to purgatory as he was likely to see in this lifetime.

Slocum pushed through the door of Magpie Maggie's saloon, and as he stepped inside, he was suddenly scared for maybe the second time in his life. All the horrors he'd already witnessed in New York paled in comparison to what awaited him. The first thing he saw was two people engaged in a vicious fight.

"Go get him, Maggie," cried one drunken thug.

The smaller of the two, Slocum saw, was a woman— an ugly, hatchet-faced hag built like a brick shithouse. Her opponent was a burly dockworker, nearly twice her size, but Magpie Maggie was no slouch. She had the docker in a headlock. She sank her teeth into the docker's ear and with one violent jerk, ripped it from his skull. Slocum watched in mute horror as the docker shrieked in pain and collapsed against a table of drunken sailors after Magpie Maggie shoved him away, the severed ear dangling proudly from between her jaws. She went back behind the bar amidst a chorus of approving cheers from the soused patrons, a rogue's gallery of Mother Nature's castoffs meaner and uglier than any of the devils he'd seen during his brief stay at Yuma prison.

Back behind the bar, Magpie Maggie deposited the freshly severed ear into a jar filled with at least two dozen other ears in various stages of decay. She screwed the cap on and put it back on a shelf behind the bar, then returned to drawing sour-smelling beer for her customers.

The ruckus in the saloon continued. Off in a corner a group of very mean-looking men were huddled around a fenced-in pit, paper money clenched in their fists. In the middle of the pit a skinny fox terrier was battling to the death with a dozen or so huge rats. The dog had one rat clenched between his jaws; the rat's blood was spraying all over the place. This seemed to excite the bettors even more, and they screamed their encouragement. The poor mongrel was losing though, futilely trying to dislodge two rats from its tail and another from its belly. Several more rats were affixed to the dog's legs, and it seemed only a matter of seconds before the rats would overwhelm the dog completely. Slocum turned away in disgust. He'd seen cockfights but this spectacle truly sickened him.

Slocum cautiously walked over to the bar, filthy saw-dust crunching under his feet. A drunk ambled up to the bar at the same time and plopped three pennies down. Magpie Maggie automatically produced a rubber tube that was attached to a beer barrel, and handed it to the drunk.

"Got to the count of ten," Magpie Maggie told him. The drunk started sucking on the rubber tube, swallowing as much of the green beer as he could as Maggie started counting. By the time she reached ten the drunk was coughing up the beer, spraying it out through his nose but still attempting to suck up more simultaneously. Maggie pulled a wooden mallet from under the bar and delivered a hard blow onto the drunk's noggin. The rubber tube slid from his mouth as he crumpled to the floor, blood oozing from the gash in his skull.

Everybody laughed at the half-dead drunk. A couple of lowlifes pounced on him like buzzards on a dead calf, rifling through his pockets for whatever they could find. Not for the first time that night could Slocum fully comprehend just how deep into the depths of depravity human beings were able to descend.

Against his better judgment, Slocum stepped up to the bar. Magpie Maggie was wiping the bar with a dirty rag.

"State your pleasure, cowboy," she said with a smile. Slocum could count her teeth on the fingers of one hand.

"Beer," he said.

"Draw one," she said to a scurvy-looking man helping her behind the bar. "And tell Michael Finn to come see me."

Slocum knew the code. Michael Finn was a Mickey Finn, any number of lethal combinations dropped into a man's beer. Three drops, Slocum knew, and a man would wake up dead. Vermin from New Orleans to Denver had tried to pull that old number on him.

The barkeep skillfully slid the doped-up mug of beer down the length of the bar, where it skidded to a stop directly before him. The aroma of chloral hydrate wafted up into his nostrils. Slocum knew he was hot on Castleberry/Steppe's trail, for the bastard had undoubtedly learned the tricks of his deadly trade in these surroundings.

"I need some information," Slocum said to Magpie Maggie.

"Never give a sucker an even break," she said automatically, wiping down the bar.

Slocum took out his tin star and slammed it on the bar.

"I'm trying to find a man named Samuel Steppe," he said. "Also known as Slats McCoy and Jedadiah

Castleberry." He pocketed the tin star.

"Never heard of him," Magpie Maggie said, squeezing beer and filth out of the rag onto the floor. "Drink your beer, stranger, mind your own p's and q's, and maybe you'll live to see the sun rise."

"Not if I drink this," Slocum snapped, and threw the beer into the hag's ugly face. For an old bag, she moved like a mountain lion, diving across the bar. Slocum lashed out with his left fist, smashing her eye with a quick but forceful blow.

Even this didn't stop the battle-ax, though; she leaped again and this time Slocum whacked her on the side of the head as hard as he could with the empty mug. Her skull was like iron. The beer mug, half an inch thick, cracked but didn't break. It had the desired effect though; the hatchet-faced fishwife collapsed like a sack of potatoes.

A big tough tried to jump Slocum from behind. It was time, Slocum decided, to teach these filthy bastards a lesson. He pulled his gun, spun on his feet and fired two shots into his attacker's heart. The thug was dead even before he hit the floor.

"Anybody else?" Slocum asked the crowd. The place was deadly silent now. The only sounds were those of the hungry rats devouring the dog's lifeless carcass.

"What is it you want, stranger?" asked a husky voice to the left. It belonged to a man sitting at a table in a darkened corner of the saloon. Slocum couldn't see his face. He sat alone, an empty glass on the table in front of him.

"I'm looking for Samuel Steppe," Slocum said. "Know him?"

"Maybe," said the man.

"Maybe means yes, most times," Slocum said. "Is this one of those times?"

"Maybe."

"Would you care for some company?" Slocum asked. "I'm buying."

"Never refuse a man who offers me a drink," the man said.

"Give me a bottle and two glasses," Slocum called over his shoulder to the bartender, never taking the gun off the man in the corner.

"Comin' up," came the reply.

Slocum slowly walked up to his new friend and got a glimpse of his face. Slocum looked into the lifeless, beady eyes of Razor Riley himself. The bartender, carrying a tray with a bottle and two shot glasses, nervously scurried up to the table and let the tray drop. He disappeared just as quickly.

Slocum approached the table but didn't sit. He poured rotgut into each of the shot glasses. Neither of them reached for the drinks.

"Samuel Steppe murdered some people in my town and shot me in the back like the yellow bastard he is," Slocum said. "And I aim to bring him back and see him dance on air."

Razor Riley growled, "How much is his hide worth to you?"

"Make me an offer."

"Steppe's a friend," Riley said. "And I charge double for friends."

"Then here's my price," Slocum said. He cocked his Colt and pointed it into the smoky gloom toward the man's head. "Your life for Steppe's whereabouts."

"You drive a hard bargain."

From the corner of his eye Slocum saw the unmistakable shadow of Magpie Maggie looming up behind him, wielding a wooden club. Slocum turned to put up his arm to block it, but was a fraction of a second too late. Magpie Maggie swung the club, connecting solidly with Slocum's ribs and knocking the wind out of him. It left him barely enough time to squeeze off a shot that merely grazed her wrinkled cheek.

Slocum fell to his knees, gasping for air, his Colt skidding away. Magpie Maggie brought the club down onto Slocum's head. He jerked his head sideways, minimizing the impact just enough to keep from crushing his skull completely. Slocum saw beautiful stars explode before his eyes. He didn't see Riley yank a lever behind the table and slam it down. The floor under Slocum disappeared. He felt himself falling through the stagnant air and hit water hard.

Rancid river water cascaded into his nostrils and down his throat. He coughed and sputtered, and the cold revived him enough to keep him conscious. He bobbed up into the scum-covered surface of the river, his head spinning. Slocum flailed his arms frantically to keep from going under again. He managed to stay afloat and not lapse into unconsciousness. With dawning horror he realized that he was floundering in a mass of tangled, decomposing corpses—Magpie Maggie's own private, soggy burial ground. Skeletal hands clutched at Slocum's throat. More slimy skeletons found their way around his legs. Slocum ripped the brittle bones off and swam dizzily away from the watery graveyard. He grabbed one of the rotting dock pilings long enough to catch his breath, then swam out into the scummy river and let himself be carried downriver by the current, until Magpie Maggie's saloon receded in the distance.

9

Slocum struggled to stay afloat, his waterlogged boots weighing him down like two anchors. Off in the distance, perhaps two hundred yards out, he spotted a rowboat drifting downriver. There appeared to be two figures working the oars. Slocum dimly remembered that it was a little late to be fishing.

He dog-paddled toward the rowboat, pushing all kinds of scummy garbage out of his way with each stroke. His bleeding skull was making him dizzier and dizzier. He'd ricocheted off a piling during his fall through the trapdoor; a couple of ribs felt cracked, maybe broken. Only the thought of his fingers curling around Magpie Maggie's gullet and choking the life out of her, watching her face turn blue and her eyes bulge out, steeled his determination to keep him from sinking down into Davy Jones's locker. As it was, he struggled for breath, swallowing what felt like gallons of the fetid river water.

This city was definitely leaving a bad taste in his mouth.

The rowboat loomed closer, and through the gray mist hanging over the water, Slocum could see two figures in heavy overcoats. They were struggling with what looked like a large sack.

"Heave, damn it," cried one, and the voice was unmistakably female.

"What does it look like I'm doing, taking a smoke?" a second voice—also female—snapped back.

"Help me," Slocum croaked when he was within ten feet of the boat.

Slocum painfully made his way to the boat and grabbed the side. The occupants were two young women of no more than twenty, wrapped up in heavy black overcoats. One looked to be a younger version of Magpie Maggie, big and ugly as sin. The second girl was kind of pretty, even through her dirt-streaked face and the woolen cap that was pulled down to her eyebrows. They still struggled to heft what Slocum now realized was a dead body, most certainly a man. There were thick ropes wrapped around him and the body was weighted down with bricks.

"Looks like we got us some company," the ugly one said as Slocum struggled to crawl into the boat.

She thrust out her oar and jabbed Slocum's chest as he hoisted himself halfway into the boat. He back-flopped into the river and heard the big one roar with laughter.

"Shouldn'ta done that, Mabel," the cute one said. "He sure was handsome."

"Lousy swimmer, though," Mabel cackled, watching Slocum's painful attempts to keep from drowning.

Slocum managed to grab the side of the boat again. He coughed up blood, then said, "You wouldn't be swimming too good if you was me, either."

Mabel slammed her oar down on Slocum's hands, though fortunately not hard enough to break his fingers. He flopped back into the river again.

"You ain't takin' a midnight swim for no reason,"

Mabel declared. "You were meant to drown and drown you will." She looked at her friend. "Clunk him good, Sally."

The pretty one grabbed her oar, then gave Slocum a second look. Their eyes locked, and even in his dazed condition, Slocum could feel the attraction. Sally's expression may have been grim, but her eyes told a different story.

"I'm not a bad man," Slocum said, gasping for air. "Don't let me die."

Nonetheless, Sally raised the oar to strike. Slocum grabbed the side of the boat a little tighter and shut his eyes, anticipating the fatal blow.

She gazed into Slocum's mug. His pathetic expression somehow managed to tug at one of her few remaining heartstrings. She clenched the oar more firmly.

"Who are you?" she asked.

"John Slocum, from Colorado," he gasped.

"Whatcha doin' in the Hudson River?" she asked.

"What are *you* doing in the Hudson River?" he countered.

"For Chrissake, finish him off or I will," Mabel put in.

Sally ignored her friend, looking at Slocum. "Give me one good reason why I shouldn't let you drown like a dirty rat," she said.

"Because, under the right circumstances, I think I could love you," Slocum said. "Though you definitely need a bath."

"I swear, Sally Balls," Mabel put in, "ain't a man south of Fourteenth Street you ain't fallen for. Give him to the fishes and let's be gone."

"Shut your pie-hole," Sally said. To Slocum she said, "Just hold on. Let me take care of this first."

She motioned to Mabel, and together they heaved the

body overboard, where it sank quickly.

"Friend of yours?" Slocum asked, still clutching the side of the boat.

"Not anymore," Mabel shot back.

Slocum chose not to pursue it any further. "I'll give you fifty dollars if you get me back on dry land."

The two rough-looking women exchanged glances. Sally shrugged, and together they helped Slocum into the small rowboat.

"I'm much obliged to you," Slocum gasped, exhausted. He started to reach for his billfold. Mabel grabbed an oar and brought it down firmly on his skull. Slocum saw newer and brighter stars. He was vaguely aware of Sally rifling through his pockets. Along with his billfold, she also found his tin star.

"Lookit this," she said to Mabel.

"Geez!" Mabel said. "He's some sort of copper. Dump him overboard."

Slocum went right back into the drink.

He felt himself sinking in the murky water, and summoned his last reserves of strength. He was able to force himself up to the surface and avoid joining his water-logged companion from the boat.

Slocum surfaced, but Mabel and Sally were already rowing frantically toward the docks. The fog had lifted enough for Slocum to see Sally Balls fling him a rope when Mabel's back was turned. Slocum wasn't one hundred percent sure—he was seeing double—but he thought he saw Sally Balls smiling at him.

Slocum managed to swim to the end of the rope. He wrapped it around his right fist and let himself be dragged through the water as the female desperadoes rowed hard toward the docks.

"Current seems kinda strong tonight," he heard Mabel

say, unaware they were hauling an additional 180-pound
load.

"Must be a storm moving in," Sally Balls said innocently, checking every now and then to make sure Slocum was
still hanging tough. He was.

As they approached the docks, Slocum released the
rope and swam off underneath. He tried to wrap his arms
around a scum-covered piling, and kept sliding back into
the water.

"This just ain't my day," Slocum muttered.

He managed to hang on long enough for Mabel and
Sally Balls to tie the rowboat to the dock and climb out.
He heard their footsteps above him on the dock, and only
when they faded in the distance did he swim to the wooden
ladder beside the rowboat.

He reached the top just in time to see Mabel and Sally
Balls disappear around a corner in the direction of Magpie
Maggie's saloon.

Slocum was quite upset that he'd been bushwhacked
by three women, Magpie Maggie included, in less than
an hour. He owed them all, and John Slocum always paid
his debts.

Since everyone he'd met in New York thus far appeared
to be members of one big crime club, these two tough
broads might know where he could find Samuel Steppe.
If not, he still wanted his money back. He followed them
down the dark, crooked cobblestone streets, staying half
a block behind them, crouching every so often behind
overflowing barrels of trash.

Mabel and Sally Balls stopped at the doorway of what
looked like a warehouse in the middle of Water Street.
He heard one of them knock twice, pause a second and
knock three more times. Yellow light spilled out onto the
gloomy street as the door creaked open. The two women

disappeared inside and the door slammed shut.

Slocum waited a few minutes, then made his way to the thick wooden door. He knocked, repeating the secret code, and sure enough the door slowly swung open. Slocum slid inside and found himself staring into Mabel's hideously ugly face.

"Remember me?" Slocum asked.

Mabel, her eyes wide with astonishment, exclaimed, "What are you still doing alive?" She looked down and saw Slocum's hand curling into a fist. As she reached for a shank tucked in her corset, she asked, "You wouldn't hit a woman, would you?"

Slocum's right fist shot out and landed flat on Mabel's wart-covered nose. In rapid-fire succession he belted her in the face four more times. She flew back and cracked her head on the wall, then sagged to the floor with blood streaming from her nostrils and mouth.

"You ain't no woman," Slocum said, and went through the pockets of her tattered overcoat for his money. The pockets were empty.

"If you're looking for your money, big man, it's stuck between my tits," Mabel mumbled.

Slocum couldn't remember a time when reaching for a woman's breasts didn't excite him, but he would rather stick his hand into a den of rattlesnakes than between Mabel's fleshy mounds. Nonetheless, he went to retrieve his cash. Mabel took the opportunity to sink her razor-sharp bicuspids into his wrist.

Her jaws were like a vise. He felt teeth touch bone. Slocum suppressed a scream, punched her three more times in the face with his free hand until her jaw unlocked. He yanked his arm away, the cash still clenched in his fist. Mabel coughed and spit out teeth. Slocum saw that she had a Colt revolver tucked into her workboot. He took it, too, replacing his Colt, which had been lost when he fell through Magpie Maggie's trapdoor.

Slocum wrapped his bandana around his wrist. Mabel's face was a bloody pulp. She wasn't going anywhere, Slocum was sure, so he made his way through the warehouse. The place seemed deserted, but Slocum could hear voices—all female, or so it sounded—behind another wooden door in the back of the warehouse. Above it a crudely lettered—not to mention misspelled—sign read "The Forty Theeves."

Slocum saw that the door was slightly ajar. He silently made his way to it and peered through.

There was a staircase that descended down into a dimly lit basement. He could make out a bunch of women scurrying around like worker ants. They were all shabbily dressed like Mabel and Sally Balls, and looked just as tough, as if they'd all been through the mill and the mill won. There were forty or so of them, ranging in age from fifteen to thirty.

Slocum crept quietly down the rickety wooden steps. Halfway there, he got a better look at the buzz of their activities, a three-ring circus of evil.

In one corner was a long wooden table loaded down with what had to be stolen goods, from diamond rings to gold picture frames. Behind the table sat two immense women built like pool tables with heads. They seemed to be tallying up the spoils of their trade, scribbling furiously in a ledger as each member of the gang—Slocum had pretty much decided that these hardened outlaw women were the Forty Thieves—lined up and deposited their hot booty on the table. This included cash money, expensive trinkets, pocket watches, even a few gold teeth.

Slocum watched as one bulldog of a woman dropped some crumpled bills and coins onto the table.

"Fifty-seven and change, Troobnik's Dry Goods," the bulldog said. "I hadda get rough with the little bastard."

One of the broads sitting behind the table looked up from her scribbling and inspected the money suspiciously.

"Troobnik is always good for at least a hundred, Gooseneck," the old bird said. "Cough it up."

"That's all there was, honest, Big Lillie," said the thief, Gooseneck Kate. "Ask Troobnik if you don't believe me."

"We don't have to," said the other woman, Gertie. "We been takin' Troobnik every week since August, and we know what kind of business he does." She rose to her feet. Standing, she looked even more formidable, all muscle and big bones. "This is the third time you come up short, Gooseneck. It's also the last time."

She pulled out a rusty old derringer and aimed it at Gooseneck Kate's chest.

"We don't tolerate skimmers, Kate," she said. "You've not been square with us."

Big Lillie put on a heavy glove, then turned and pulled a red-hot poker out of a roaring fireplace.

"I wasn't skimming, honest," Gooseneck Kate said to the other big broad.

"Way we got it figured," said Gertie, "you owe us three hundred bucks."

Gooseneck Kate swallowed hard. "It ain't so. I swear," she stammered.

"How much was it?" Big Lillie asked, waving the poker. The end was glowing orange from the fire.

"Kiss me arse," Gooseneck Kate snapped, trying to sound tough, but there was clearly fear in her voice. She tried to run but was easily intercepted by half a dozen of her associates. Gooseneck Kate's arms were pinned behind her back and she was forced to face Big Lillie, who now stood before her.

"You stole from us," Big Lillie said, and spit on the glowing tip of the poker. She watched it sizzle. "You have to be punished."

"I swear, Lillie, it wasn't nothing, just a few nickels and dimes."

Lillie placed the tip of the hot poker directly under Gooseneck Kate's nose.

"I don't believe you," Lillie said softly. "Now open your mouth and say 'Aaah.' "

Knowing she had no other choice, Gooseneck Kate dutifully opened her mouth wide and shut her eyes. The last thing Slocum saw before he turned away was Lillie shoving the burning poker in the vicinity of Gooseneck Kate's open mouth. This was followed by a bloodcurdling scream of agony; the rest was left to Slocum's imagination.

In the process of turning away from the grisly scene, Slocum shifted his weight. The rotting wooden step cracked in half, sending Slocum tumbling down to the bottom of the stairs.

Forty heads turned as Slocum, curled into the fetal position, came to rest on the dirt floor of the warehouse basement. The place was quiet except for Gooseneck Kate's weak moans of pain.

Slocum opened his eyes to see Sally Balls work her way through the crowd and look down at him, shaking her head sympathetically.

"You stupid jerk," she said.

10

Slocum opened his eyes. The world was upside down.

His first hope was that perhaps the Forty Thieves were all standing on their heads. When he felt the thick ropes cutting into his wrists and ankles, he knew at once that he was suspended upside down from a baling hook hanging from the ceiling. His body was swathed in chains, making any movement impossible. His hands were securely tied behind his back.

Slocum, even with his world topsy-turvy, saw the battered bloody face of Mabel glaring at him. Glancing to his left, Slocum also realized that he was not alone in this predicament. Gooseneck Kate was suspended next to him, and was much worse off. She appeared to be quite dead, her charred lips and mouth agape and a slow but steady stream of blood oozed out into a puddle on the floor.

The Forty Thieves were all congregated in front of Slocum. They all looked like the type who would gleefully pull the wings off a fly, then eat the fly for good measure.

"Whadda we do with him?" Gashouse Gertie asked Big Lillie.

"Whatever it is," said Mabel with black hate in her eyes, "I want the first crack at him. Promise me, Gashouse."

"Sure, but we don't do nothin' until Steppe sees him," Gashouse Gertie said. At the mention of the name, Slocum lifted his head. Mabel lurched forward and kicked Slocum in the face.

Sally Balls stared wistfully at Slocum, knowing that to help him would mean almost certain death. Too bad— even with his face cut and bloodied, the cowboy was sort of handsome. Sally knew that Slocum would be a dead man in a matter of minutes unless. . . .

"What the hell does Steppe want with him?" Lillie asked, slapping a blackjack against her palm. The other Forty Thieves were all brandishing weapons, from wooden clubs studded with nails, to knives, to the latest fashions from Smith and Wesson.

"This sniveling sack of snakeshit's been askin' one too many questions around town," Gashouse Gertie said. "Sam wants to ask Sheriff Shithead here some of his own." She played Slocum's tin star between her fingers like a coin.

Slocum heard the wooden basement door crash open. He saw three men descend the staircase and approach him. One face was instantly recognizable, even from Slocum's angle. It was Jedadiah Castleberry—alias Samuel Steppe— the man who'd shot him in the back; the reason Slocum was now hanging upside down and his brain felt like it was going to explode.

"I must say, I admire your tenacity," Castleberry/Steppe said to Slocum. "Though there's often a very thin line between tenacity and stupidity."

Steppe grabbed the rope and started swinging Slocum gently.

"I'm flattered, Slocum, that you think highly enough of me to pursue me across half the country. Things were getting a little hot for me in New York, so I decided to head West for a cooling off period; otherwise I'd have never darkened your door at all."

"You're under arrest," Slocum rasped. "For the murders of James Wilson "Jug" Jackson, age 61; Mrs. Ulysses Morris Leonard, age 58; Mr. Clarence Henry the Third, age 49; and one half-breed Sioux, Herbert Pissing Horse, age unknown."

Steppe grinned from ear to ear and turned to walk away, then grabbed Slocum by the hair and jerked his body upwards. The chains around Slocum's chest squeezed his rib cage painfully. A million needles pierced his scalp as Steppe yanked at Slocum's hair.

"I prefer to choose my own friends, Slocum," Steppe bellowed, his eyes blazing with hellfire. "I can't have half-assed hayseeds chasing me around my own backyard. It's bad for my digestion."

Slocum said, "Maybe it's a guilty conscience that's puttin' you off your food."

Steppe released the rope and walked away. Slocum rocked back and forth like a bloody pendulum. Steppe, to Slocum's surprise, curled his arm around Sally Balls's waist and pulled her close. He produced a silk handkerchief and wiped her dirty left cheek clean, then kissed it. Sally smiled, but Slocum could see by her slight flinch that there was little love there.

"Sally's my girl," Steppe said. "Does whatever I tell her to."

He pulled a pearl-handled knife from his pocket and handed it to her.

"Kill him," Steppe said. "Kill him the way you make love, my sweet: nice and slow. Then dump his stinking carcass into the river and let's get back to business."

Sally knew that even the slightest hesitation would make everyone suspicious, something she couldn't afford right now. She grabbed the knife from Steppe and slowly approached Slocum, who looked up at her with wide eyes. She knew she had no choice but to finish him off per Steppe's command, and tried to decide which part of his body she could stab that would hurt the least.

The decision was made for her.

"I wanna kill him first," Mabel cried out, pure venom in her voice. "You promised, Gashouse." She came forward, a pigsticker the size of New Jersey in her fist.

Steppe turned to Gashouse Gertie. "Is this true, Gertie?"

Gashouse Gertie's face turned the color of clam chowder. She knew that Steppe didn't like it when members of a gang under his control made promises without his approval, even a boss such as herself.

"You know I'd never do that, Sam," Gashouse Gertie gasped. "Honest. I—"

"You're getting sloppy, Gertie," Steppe said, and grabbed her gullet, sinking his fingers into her flesh. With his other hand he cracked her back and forth across her ugly puss until blood spurted from her mouth. Gashouse Gertie, to her credit, took her punishment stoically.

Steppe shoved her aside and turned to Mabel, her face bloodied and puffy from Slocum's punches.

"He did this to you?" Steppe asked, inspecting Mabel's face.

She nodded.

Steppe motioned toward Slocum. "What'd you have in mind?" he asked her.

"The unkindest cut of all," Mabel said, plucking the tip of her pigsticker. "I'm gonna cut his pecker off and feed it to my mutt."

"Splendid," Steppe remarked. "The job is yours."

Mabel grinned; it looked like a smile on a contented warthog.

She walked up to Slocum's gently swaying form. She slowly pulled down the zipper of his pants.

"You're gonna be hittin' them high notes pretty good when I get through with you," she croaked, reaching into his pants and searching for Slocum's most valued organ. Regrettably, she found it.

Mabel whistled shrilly, and a mangy terrier nearly as ugly as she was trotted in dutifully. She snapped her fingers and the dog sat about two feet away from Slocum, wagging its tail, raising a small cloud of dust across the dirty floor, and drooling hungrily.

"Rover's got hisself a taste for human blood," she said to Slocum, who wanted desperately to pass out. The thought of his manhood becoming some doggie's dinner didn't please him much.

Before the not-so-delicate operation could begin, the cellar door flew open and within seconds the place was flooded with men in blue uniforms, swinging billy clubs and cracking heads.

"You lowlifes are all under arrest," a man cried in a brogue thicker than Irish stew. Slocum recognized the voice. It was Flannery, the detective he'd slugged at the police station.

Women screamed, cops bashed heads, and Slocum saw Steppe grab Sally Balls by the arm and disappear from sight into the violent melee. Mabel also took flight as the police began the raid of the Forty Thieves' headquarters.

Even hanging upside down Slocum could see the black

eye he'd given Flannery as the Irish cop suddenly loomed before him.

"My first instinct is to leave you to hang, Slocum," Flannery said.

"What's your second instinct?" Slocum asked. He was never so glad to see anybody.

Flannery grunted. "MacDougall," he snapped at a uniformed policeman who had just finished clubbing one of the Forty Thieves.

"Yessir?" MacDougall asked, dropping the battered woman to the floor.

"Cut this man down," Flannery ordered, "and don't be doing it gently."

MacDougall produced a knife from his coat and did as Flannery asked, grabbing the rope that held Slocum suspended and cutting through it.

Stumpy Malarkey, the livery driver, suddenly appeared and stood alongside Flannery. MacDougall managed to slice through the thick rope, and Slocum slammed to the floor, headfirst.

"What might you be thinking about our Mister Slocum, Stumpy?" Flannery asked the pint-sized Malarkey.

"I'd say he's looked better," Stumpy said.

"Take him home and put him to bed," Slocum heard Flannery say to Stumpy. Slocum rolled himself into a ball on the floor and became unconscious.

11

Slocum only wanted to sleep. He was lying in a bed in the back room of Stumpy Malarkey's East Side tenement flat, nursing his wounds with Stumpy and his wife Edna's help. Stumpy had loaded the badly battered Slocum into his cab and taken him home, where Edna had cleaned his wounds, taped his ribs, and put him into bed. Slocum had been out for two days, floating in and out of consciousness. He vaguely remembered a doctor with thick gray eyebrows poking and prodding him and pronouncing him bruised but otherwise all right. Needless to say, Slocum had been separated from his bankroll somewhere along the line. Mabel's gun was gone as well.

"What he needs more than anything is bed rest," Slocum vaguely remembered the old sawbones saying. "The ribs are badly bruised but not broken. None of his other wounds seem too severe."

That was, Slocum calculated through his feverish mind, two days ago. He was fully conscious now, and here was Edna, trying to nourish him with her tasteless Irish fare. Slocum had managed to keep down some beef broth earlier in the day, but his stomach rebelled at the mere thought of solid food.

"Now open wide," Edna Malarkey instructed, holding a fork with a soggy piece of corned beef impaled on it inches from his mouth. "We've got to eat if we want to get all better."

"What's this 'we'?" Slocum asked. "All of a sudden you're my deputy?"

"I'm the Lord's deputy," Edna responded.

Slocum pushed the fork away.

"I'm not too hungry, Missus Malarkey," he said.

"Eat it," she ordered, jabbing the meat at him.

"No, sorry ma'am," Slocum said. "It'll come up faster than I can get it down."

Mrs. Malarkey dropped the fork onto the plate and tossed them impatiently onto the serving tray. "You're a very stubborn man, Mr. Slocum," she said. Edna Malarkey was even shorter than her husband, a chubby elf with a face pink with peasant health. "You wouldn't by any chance be a Catholic, would you?"

" 'Fraid not," Slocum said. "Why do you ask?"

"Because you've got the temperament," she said. "Traveling all the way from Colorado indeed. It's a good, solid lass that'll be keeping you home and out of trouble, John Slocum. Only through the mercy of our good Lord Jesus Christ are you alive today. It's His way of saying the time is ripe to start changing your ways."

There was a single knock on the bedroom door, then Stumpy came in and announced, "Detective Flannery is here, and he'd like to see Mister Slocum."

"He might as well," Edna snapped, grabbing the serving tray that held Slocum's uneaten dinner. "If it's not food he's wanting, maybe it's company." She carried the tray out of the room. Flannery, looking grimly amused, stepped inside. Edna closed the door behind them.

Flannery removed his bowler hat, slapped it on a chest of drawers, and sat on the edge of the bed. He glared at Slocum through one good eye; the other was black and swollen shut.

"Hell of a shiner you got there," Slocum said. "How'd you get it?"

"Some lawman from Colorado gave it to me," Flannery said casually.

"What's on your mind?" Slocum asked.

"I want you to go home," Flannery said. "Soon as you're well. I've neither the manpower nor the desire to keep you alive during your holiday here."

"Don't worry about me," Slocum said. "You do your job and I'll do mine."

"I can't be having that, Slocum," Flannery said. "Samuel Steppe is a dangerous man with some powerful connections to Tammany Hall. He's personally protected by Boss Penderblast himself, the grand poobah of the Fourth Ward. Penderblast barks, and the police in this town play dead. He's barking now, Slocum, for your hide . . . and Penderblast's bite is much worse than his bark."

"You tellin' me that Steppe's got the law on his side?" Slocum asked.

"Samuel Steppe runs most of the vice downtown," Flannery said. "That includes controlling all of the gangs like the Forty Thieves, the Dead Rabbits, and the Bowery Boys. Murder, robbery, prostitution, gambling, extortion— Steppe controls it and shares the spoils with Penderblast, who protects him from the law."

"Sounds like you're all in bed together," Slocum said.

"Perhaps it does," Flannery said, and stood up. He grabbed his bowler. "But there's one thing you need to know, John. You're not the only honest lawman in the

United States of America. Yes, Tammany has two thirds of the police department in its pocket, but me, and others like me, we're the one third they don't have."

Flannery walked to the door, then stopped and continued. "You leave Samuel Steppe to me, Slocum. I've been trying to crucify the devil for ten years, and I'm getting closer to putting him in the Tombs—that's a jail that all criminals fear—than ever before. I'll not be needing any help from the likes of you. Just get better, go home, and forget about this insane quest of yours. To make sure you do, I'm posting some men at the entrance of the building in case you had yourself any fancy ideas about slipping away. They'll also be waiting to escort you to Grand Central Station and putting you personally on the train."

"I'm a pretty fair hand with a gun, Flannery," Slocum said. "Maybe I can be of some help."

"No," Flannery said, in a tone Slocum knew to be final. "You'd kill Steppe first chance you get. Not that he doesn't deserve it, mind you, but in my town, we let the law take its due course. That means a trial and a jury of his peers."

"I know the law, too, Flannery," Slocum said. "And that means we got ourselves a problem."

"And what might that problem be?"

"I don't know what Steppe's wanted for here," Slocum said, "but it's murder in Colorado, and murder's pretty high up on my list of hangin' offenses. I aim to bring him back dead or alive, Flannery. It's my job."

"I'll make a deal with you, Slocum," Flannery said. "After we capture and convict the wretch, you'll get an invitation to his execution."

Flannery removed a train ticket from his breast pocket and tossed it on the bed. "Until that happy day," he said, "I don't want to see hide nor hair of you anywhere near my city. You defend your territory and I'll defend mine."

"He gave you the slip once, when he came to my town and bushwhacked me," Slocum said. "He'll do it again."

"He won't," Flannery insisted.

"Come on, Flannery," Slocum said. "You don't need him that bad. There's probably hundreds like him leaving trails of slime all over New York. To you, getting Steppe is nothing more than a feather in your cap, maybe a promotion to captain. To me, seein' that rope stretch his neck like warm taffy is also sendin' a message to every back-shootin', back-stabbin' Yankee bastard who spits in the eye of the law. I got to make an example of him."

Flannery shrugged. "The choice is yours. You can leave on a train tomorrow or in a meat wagon destined for a pauper's grave in potter's field. In layman's terms, Slocum, get out of town."

He opened the door and stepped out. As he started to close it behind him, Slocum called out, "Flannery?"

Flannery turned and looked exasperated, raising one thick eyebrow. "Yes, Mr. Slocum?"

"By sundown?"

12

Sally Balls paid Slocum a visit about an hour after Flannery left.

Slocum awoke from a fitful doze to see her standing at the foot of the bed. She was cleaned up now, her hair shiny and pinned up in a severe bun. She clutched a pink umbrella, looking quite stylish, nothing like the dirty scalawag who'd saved his life days earlier.

"Not bad for a street urchin," Slocum said.

"First impressions ain't always reliable," Sally Balls said with a smile.

"Why'd you help me?" Slocum asked.

"Something in your eyes," Sally said. "Told me you were on the up-and-up."

"Is that good?"

"It is in my book," she said.

"Mind if I flip through your pages someday?" Slocum asked.

"Don't get snotty, Slocum," Sally said. "Steppe knows you're still alive. You've got to leave today if you want to leave at all."

"This may be an odd question," Slocum said, "but why are you here?"

"To warn you," she said, tension etched on her pretty features now. "If Steppe knew I was here, I'd be dead by dawn."

"Thought you were his girlfriend," Slocum said.

"His opinion, not mine," Sally Balls replied. "Two years ago, Flannery and his men caught me and another of the Forty Thieves robbing a pawnshop on the East Side. The owner got nervous, and Sadie the Ox beat him to death with her bare fists. Sadie got the rope, but Flannery fixed it so I'd go free if I agreed to spy on Steppe's criminal organization. Steppe's only one or two rungs under Boss Penderblast. He's the one Flannery's trying to nail to the wall."

"And he's using you as bait," Slocum said.

"It was either that or the gallows. I'm from the streets, Slocum. I'd've ended up dead a lot sooner if Flannery hadn't given me a second chance."

"How many men does Penderblast have?" Slocum asked. The enormity of this criminal empire was slowly making an impression on him. It was beginning to dawn on Slocum that taking on Penderblast and Steppe was akin to fighting the entire Cherokee nation singlehandedly.

"More than you'll ever be able to handle," she said. "Now that Steppe knows you're running around loose, he's at a place where an army couldn't get to him."

"Tell me where and let me worry about the rest," Slocum said.

"Oh no," she said. "Flannery warned me you'd start asking questions."

"Seems to me," Slocum said, "a woman in your position wants Steppe dead more'n I do."

"What of it?"

"Tell me where to find him," Slocum said, "and I give you my word he'll never bother you or anyone else again."

"If I tell you," she said, "you'll die. It's as simple as that."

"I haven't died yet, and I've sampled every torture of the damned your fair city has to offer."

"No," she said.

"Money, then," Slocum said. "Name your price. I'm sure you've done it before."

Her face suddenly turned hard and Slocum was sure she'd go for his throat. Instead, she made for the door and grabbed the doorknob, clenching it tightly.

"Say that again," she said softly, her voice tinged with menace, "and I'll rip your eyes out."

"Tell me or get the hell out," Slocum said. "Go back to your gutter and wallow in the mud. Maybe someday you'll get promoted to maggot."

"You stink, mister," Sally Balls said coldly. Slocum could see the hard years of slum life etched in her face. It was the same look Midnight Rose got whenever Slocum raised her dander. "If I wasn't a lady, I'd make you dead for that."

Slocum snorted. "Don't know many ladies who dump bodies into the river at high midnight."

"I didn't kill him, but take my word for it, he had it coming all the same," she snapped. "Now you listen to me, saddletramp. You don't know me, you don't know anything about me. I'll not be having you loosenin' your filthy lips at my expense."

Slocum leaped from the bed and faced her.

"Filthy lips for filthy women," Slocum hissed.

Sally Balls swung at him like lightning, her hand a claw with razor-sharp fingernails ready to carve deep gashes in his face. Slocum grabbed her wrist before she could connect, twisted it, and threw her down on the bed. Sally Balls sprang up and pounced, but Slocum was ready. His hand shot out and covered her face. He thrust and sent her slamming back onto the bed. He jumped on top of her and pinned her wrists to the bed, straddling her.

Sally Balls spat in his face. The gob splattered perfectly in his left eye. She flailed her legs, striking Slocum in the back. This was one tough filly.

"Dirty stinkin' cowboy bastard," Sally Balls hissed, struggling mightily.

The door opened. Edna Malarkey, looking worried, hands clenched at her substantial bosom, stood there.

Both Slocum and Sally Balls stopped their tussling and looked at her.

Slocum said, "Would you kindly leave us alone for a moment, Mrs. Malarkey?"

Edna closed the door without comment. Sally Balls seized the moment. She freed her left hand from Slocum's clutch and punched him squarely in the jaw. It was a surprisingly forceful punch for so small a woman, stunning Slocum just long enough for Sally Balls to wriggle free. She chopped him on the back of the neck, and Slocum crashed face-first into the bed.

Sally Balls stood and started straightening herself up.

"I thought you were different," she said, breathing heavily and fixing her hair. "You're just another . . . *man.*"

Slocum didn't move. He moaned in pain.

"Okay, bigshot," Sally Balls said. "Steppe is leading the Forty Thieves on a robbery at midnight. There's a fortune in precious silks from the Far East. The boat docked this morning. The *Evangeline.* West Street and Canal."

She finished primping and walked to the door again.

"I hope they kill you," she said, and left.

Edna scurried into the room. Slocum looked slightly dazed as Edna gently examined his sore chin with her fingers, clucking her tongue in sympathy.

"I heard everything, Mr. Slocum," Edna said, taking a wet cloth and wiping his forehead. "God forgive me, but you had it coming."

"I had to get her mad so'd she tell me," he muttered. "It was the only way."

"Mr. Slocum," Edna said, "what you don't know about women could fill the Atlantic."

"Maybe," Slocum said, and called for Stumpy. He appeared in the doorway, a napkin tucked into his shirt. A half-eaten turkey leg was clenched in his fist.

"You got any rope?" Slocum asked. "About forty feet's worth?"

Stumpy said, "What for?"

"You're going to lower me out the back window into the courtyard," he said. "There's two policemen out front watching for me."

"But we're on the fourth floor. Sounds dangerous, John," Stumpy said.

"It gets worse," Slocum said. "After you lower me down, Edna's going to lower *you* down."

"And why is that?"

"I need you to take me someplace," Slocum said.

"Someplace where?" Stumpy asked suspiciously. His appetite was suddenly gone.

"Canal Street," Slocum said, "But first I'll need to get a gun. Know where can I get one?"

"I'm beginning to wish I'd never picked you up," Stumpy said wearily, and went in search of the rope.

"Begging your pardon, sir," Stumpy said, snapping the reins against his horses' rumps. The carriage careened through the dark, crooked streets of lower Manhattan. "But when I last looked, you was only one man."

"It was the best I could do," Slocum said back, dropping some bullets into the chamber of the old but still reliable Colt he'd bought from a mean-looking thug in a Bowery saloon Stumpy had taken him to earlier. Stumpy had a very good reason for not wanting Slocum to die—he'd loaned Slocum the twenty dollars to buy it.

"Then let me turn back and let's forget this foolishness," Stumpy said, wary of being in this part of town at this time of night. A thick, chilly fog was settling in over the streets of New York, denser than on the moors of Yorkshire.

"Just leave me on Canal Street," Slocum said, slapping the barrel of the Colt back into place and spinning it. "Scoot on home and hide under your bed if you're so scared."

"Stumpy Malarkey ain't scared of man nor beast," Stumpy said. "As long as there ain't too many of both at one time. That's what you're up against, lad."

"Reckon that's my worry," Slocum said.

"Reckon that's my worry as well," Stumpy said. "The missus has taken a likin' to your honest ways. 'Don't let no harm come to him, Horace' she says to me, as though she's the one who's roaming around Satan's playground in the black of night."

"Is that your given name? Horace?"

"Me mother gave it to me, but I never asked for it," he replied. "Always hated a name that started with 'hor'."

"So much for the luck of the Irish," Slocum said.

Malarkey slowed the carriage to a stop on a fog-shrouded street corner, the sickly yellow skein of the streetlight barely cutting through it. The stench of rotting fish and burning coal filled their nostrils.

"Welcome to Canal Street," Stumpy said.

Slocum jumped out of the carriage and tried to peer through the fog. "Which way's the docks?"

"Follow your nose," Stumpy said. "If you're smart, you'll hold it, too." He pointed west, then snapped the reins again. The carriage disappeared into the night fog.

"Good luck, Slocum," he heard Stumpy cry out. "May the good Lord drop what He's doing and look over yer."

13

Slocum skulked through a shantytown adjacent to the piers. He'd never seen anything quite like it before short of the docks of New Orleans. Tar paper shacks and crudely constructed lean-tos filled with gaunt, pale faces lined West Street; the few blocks between Canal and West Streets were a pathetic exercise in squalor. Slocum kept one hand clenched on the handle of his gun, nestled firmly under his belt. He dodged the malnourished, disease-ridden waterfront denizens who grabbed at him with bony fingers. Slocum was able to shake them loose until one, an emaciated man with a scrawny beard who reeked of grain alcohol, latched onto his arm.

"Pennies, sir, just a few pennies," the man croaked.

Slocum pulled his Colt and slammed the handle onto the man's head. His grip loosened and he fell to the ground. With this, the dirty crowd parted like the Red Sea.

Slocum crouched behind a dilapidated plywood shack. The *Evangeline,* sure enough, was docked two hundred yards away. Slocum could see a few crewmen on watch through the fog; otherwise, things seemed quiet. Slocum

estimated that he had about five minutes or so before
Steppe and the Forty Thieves would arrive. He wanted
to be on board the schooner when that happened.

But getting aboard was the tricky part.

Slocum made his way to one of the tar paper shacks.
Inside was a prune of a man, in a ratty, moth-eaten overcoat and ripped woolen cap. A rummy, Slocum knew,
judging by the man's swollen red nose. A burlap sack
filled with half-rotten potatoes sat next to him.

The man raised pink eyes at Slocum, ready to give up
his stash.

"If it's me potatoes you want, take 'em and let an
old man die in peace the way God sees fit," the old
weasel said.

"It ain't your potatoes I want," Slocum said. "It's your
coat."

Slocum tossed the old man a silver dollar he'd kept
sewn up inside his belt, the only currency the Forty Thieves
hadn't gotten.

"We got a deal?" Slocum asked.

The old fart half laughed, half wheezed, and said, "Hell,
sonny, I'll even give you me longjohns."

"Just give me the hat and we'll call it even," Slocum
said.

Slocum, wearing the seedy overcoat and wool cap,
approached the gangplank of the *Evangeline*. He had
a burlap sack filled with pieces of brick slung over his
shoulder. For the occasion, he'd rubbed ashes on his
face, looking even more like a rumpot veteran of the
Seven Seas.

"Ahoy, mates," Slocum called to a duo of burly crewmen
on watch. "Seaman Patrick Michael O'Toole reportin'
for duty."

"On whose orders?" asked one of the sailors suspiciously. Few men sailed on the *Evangeline* willingly.

"I couldn't be saying, mates," Slocum said, coating his words with a bit of the brogue. "The yank just told me the *Evangeline*. Said he needed some hands for a voyage to San Francisco. Well, then, here I be."

"San Francisco?" cried the other sailor. "Why, it's Hong Kong we're headed for when after we unload tomorrow."

"You don't tell me!" Slocum said, making his way up the gangplank. "Hong Kong, now there's a port I've always wanted to see. Slant-eyed China dolls shaped like hourglasses is what they tell me."

The two sailors started laughing. "Not this trip, you miserable fool," one of them said. He tossed Slocum a few coins. "Fill your belly with rum, chum. Now off with ye."

Slocum swung and knocked one of the sailors over the head with the burlap bag. Before the second sailor could even react, Slocum slugged him in the head until he, too, fell unconscious to the deck.

Slocum dragged the bodies away and hid them under a smelly, mildewed tarp. Slocum's luck continued: other than these two, the rest of the crew apparently had shore leave or had been paid to become scarce.

He made his way down to the cargo hold. There were what looked to be hundreds of crates stacked one on top of the other. He saw one crate that appeared to have already been pried open. Slocum lifted the lid and peered inside. Sure enough, it was filled with precious silks of all colors.

Obviously, one of Steppe's cohorts had checked the goods before the robbery to ensure that the cargo included everything it was supposed to.

Slocum heard the clomping of heavy boots on the deck above, followed by loud voices, that were getting louder. Then there were steps of what sounded like a hundred men descending into the cargo hold.

Slocum thought fast.

The crate of silks would just about hold him, he decided, with maybe even an inch or two to spare. He climbed in and buried himself under three feet of silk, pulling the lid over him.

The voices became crystal-clear. Slocum had company.

The lid above him was torn away. Slocum lay completely still, not even breathing.

"What did I tell you, sir?" asked a voice husky from years of rotgut whiskey. "The finest silks money can buy—or a man can steal." He cackled and the sound was like fingernails on a chalkboard.

"All right," a second voice said. Slocum was certain it was Steppe. "Load them onto the wagons and be quick about it, or I'll whale the tar out of the lot of you."

"Yessir," came the reply, and the lid was replaced. Slocum let out an audible gasp, muffled by the silks.

Moments later, Slocum felt himself—and the crate— being lifted and carried up the steps to the deck.

"I'd like to see the size of the worms that spun this silk," Slocum heard one of his carriers comment. "Weighs a ton, it does."

"That means it's of high quality," said a second.

"And what might ye be knowing about silk, pecker-head," replied the first. "Ye've never been any closer to it than a hog to a bathtub."

Slocum was carried down the gangplank and eventually onto the back of what Slocum assumed was a wagon. Then more crates were piled on top of him with bone-jarring efficiency, and Slocum knew he was sealed up in his own private coffin. Fortunately, breathing wouldn't be a major problem, but laying in a wooden crypt darker than the night for more than a few hours would be. Slocum tried to relax and convince himself that the situation was just temporary, but total panic was right around the corner.

The wagon started moving; Slocum heard the clip-clop of horse's hooves on cobblestone. The gentle swaying of the wagon and the forward motion helped quell the panic Slocum felt at being buried alive.

"I'm getting too old for this shit," Slocum muttered to himself. Then the wagon hit a pothole in the street that Slocum could feel in his kidneys.

The wagon came to an abrupt halt, Slocum calculated, some thirty or so blocks later. They'd headed north, he knew, for the wagon had gone across what he remembered to be Canal Street, then turned a sharp left uptown— Stumpy called everything north of the docks uptown. Up usually meant north, though in New York, Slocum reasoned, anything was possible.

Slocum could feel the crates piled atop him being hastily unloaded and hauled somewhere else. Slocum prayed they planned to unpack the fruits of their illicit labors tonight and not next week, leaving him to a slow death.

He was dropped, not gently, onto the floor. Slocum felt the cheap iron fillings rattle in his mouth.

"Hurry now and let's be gone," Steppe yelled.

Slocum heard the squeals and teeth scraping of a rat trying to gnaw through a small knothole on the right side of the crate. The knothole was barely within reaching distance.

"Beat it," Slocum hissed, slamming his palm against the knothole and knocking the varmint back. The scrawny rat was single-minded of purpose though, and attacked the knothole again. He quickly made excellent progress, judging from the size of the hole. Slocum had seen a huge rat in Denver slither through a penny-sized hole in a cracker barrel. If not repelled, this furry bastard would chew his way into the crate and make Slocum's life miserable.

"Little shit," Slocum hissed, and poked the barrel of his gun squarely into the rat's snout. The rat viciously attacked the barrel, and Slocum had to keep thrusting it through the knothole to shake him loose.

An unshaven, thick-witted thug moving crates nearby happened to notice the commotion. He slowly sauntered over, blinking a few times. No doubt about it; someone was in the crate poking a gun at the rat.

"What's this now?" the thug exclaimed, then tore off the lid.

Slocum was up and swinging, delivering a well-placed right hook to the thug's jaw. It was made of glass. He pitched backward into a pile of crates.

The next second or two were a blur. Slocum saw all activity cease, then focused on Steppe standing on a pile of crates maybe twenty yards away, a tall Napoleon ruling over his troops.

"Shit," Slocum heard Steppe mutter, and saw fear in his eyes.

"Anybody move, he's a dead man," Slocum said to the stunned crowd, training the barrel on Steppe's heart. He looked at Steppe. "You're under arrest, you yellow bastard."

Several of Steppe's goons made moves for their weapons. Steppe calmly held his arms out, restraining them momentarily.

"What will it take to buy your friendship?" Steppe asked.

Slocum stepped out of the crate. At the same time, a two-legged river rat made a dive for him. Slocum pivoted and spat hellfire from the trusty Colt. A red hole opened in the man's forehead. Slocum pivoted back and blasted down a second lowlife who was foolish enough to draw on him. Slocum pumped two shots into the man's belly, the first to kill and the second for practice. He had the gun back on Steppe in a blink of an eye.

"I ain't for sale," Slocum said. "Maybe the only one in this town."

"You'll never walk out of here alive," Steppe hissed.

"If I don't, you don't either."

"I have ten thousand dollars in my pocket, Slocum," Steppe said. "It's yours if you'll just go the hell away."

"Let's see it," Slocum said.

Steppe reached into his inside coat pocket and pulled out a big green wad of cash.

"Toss it here," Slocum said.

Steppe tossed the banded ball of money. It hit the floor and rolled neatly to Slocum's feet.

"Now you're also under arrest for trying to bribe an officer of the law," Slocum said, kicking the cash into a corner. Half a dozen rats descended on it, chewing it to a pulp.

"I used to think you were just stupid, Slocum," Steppe said. "Now I know for sure you're stupid *and* you're crazy."

"Climb down off your mountain, Hannibal," Slocum said. "I'm takin' you home."

He fired a shot at Steppe's feet. Steppe didn't even flinch.

A second goon, standing next to his dead friend, went for his gun. Slocum spun, fired, and made the man go away. Steppe dived off the pile of crates into the darkness of the warehouse. At the same moment, the warehouse door flew open and a wave of blue suits cascaded in, led by the intrepid Detective Kevin Flannery.

"Nobody move," Flannery cried, and then all hell broke loose.

14

Slocum's first instinct was to shoot, but then he recognized the square-jawed Flannery and relaxed his trigger finger. At the same time, Flannery drew his pistol and aimed at the first figure he saw—John Slocum.

Flannery didn't have Slocum's discipline with a gun. He squeezed off a shot. Slocum hit the floor, and the shot slammed into the chest of a gang member standing behind him.

"You peckerhead, it's me," Slocum yelled at Flannery.

A shot rang out, and a bullet whizzed over Flannery's head. He dived to the ground, rolled behind a stack of crates, and came up shooting. Cops and robbers alike also started diving for cover, and then the gunplay began in earnest.

Slocum scrambled behind a stack of crates. He saw three cops go down in the opening barrage. Slocum started firing at the men shooting at Flannery's men. All around him, guns belched streaks of orange in the relative darkness of the warehouse. Bodies fell from behind stacks of crates and from the catwalks above them, crashing to the ground with bone-crunching thuds.

Flannery poked his head up from behind a crate only to see a shotgun barrel five feet from his face. Suddenly, a six-shooter roared and the shotgun and its owner fell to the floor. Slocum rose up from behind the crate, cockily blowing smoke from his Colt. Flannery's eyes squinted with recognition.

"What the bloody hell are you doing here, Slocum?" Flannery shouted.

"Same as you," Slocum cried out. "Upholding the law. Had everything under control, too, 'til you blundered in!"

"You're a lunatic," Flannery yelled over the gunfire, then ducked as bullets peppered the floor around him.

Slocum also crouched back down and quickly reloaded his Colt. He popped up again to see Flannery firing at the men on the catwalk above. Slocum saw a man on the catwalk grab his leg and pitch forward over the railing and plummet to the floor. Slocum squeezed off a shot and hit the falling man in the belly, finishing the job.

"Where's Steppe?" Flannery called out to Slocum.

"Most likely getting away, thanks to you," Slocum called back, reloading.

Slocum saw Steppe and a few of his men rush out a side door. He turned his gun on them and fired, hitting one of them in the side. Steppe and the others disappeared into the fog.

Slocum squatted and duck-walked through the maze of crates, dodging bullets. He took refuge behind a stack of crates a few yards from the open door, fired off a shot or two, then was up and running out, Flannery right behind him.

Steppe and two of his men jumped into a wagon. One of them slid into the seat and grabbed the reins, cracking them and spurring the horses into action.

Slocum ran out into the street and fired in their general direction as they vanished into the foggy night.

"Damn," Slocum cried. "Goddamn!" He holstered his gun and stomped angrily in a circle.

"You cocked it up, Flannery," Slocum bellowed in Flannery's face. "I had him dead center, six ways from Sunday, and you cocked it all up!"

It was Flannery's turn to be angry now. His face was purple with rage.

"And I told you to go home," Flannery bellowed back. "Six months planning this raid and I finally had Steppe red-handed. So don't you be screaming at me about cocking anything up, you dime-novel desperado!"

They stood glaring at each other, panting heavily.

"Get the hell out of my city," Flannery said, seething with anger. "You're not good enough to play cowboys and Indians here."

"Good enough to save your miserable hide," Slocum shot back.

"That's right," Flannery agreed. "And I never even said thank you."

He lashed out and belted Slocum solidly on the jaw, hard enough to send Slocum sprawling onto the street.

"Thank you!" Flannery said. "Now go home."

Slocum sat up, shook his head a few times, then rubbed his jaw. It would definitely be sore, and very soon.

They heard the clattering of horses's hooves behind him and turned to see Stumpy Malarkey and his buggy pull up in front of him.

"We'd better hurry if you want to catch him, John Slocum," Stumpy said.

Slocum sprinted onto the seat beside Stumpy. Flannery tried to follow him, but a crushing haymaker from Slocum on Flannery's good eye sent him tumbling backwards onto the street. He was stunned just long enough for Slocum to grab the reins. He stood and jerked the reins and yelled "Eee-haw!" The horse reared up proudly and galloped off in pursuit, nearly jolting Slocum and Stumpy out of the seat.

"Sweet Jesus and Mother Mary," Stumpy said, amazed. "She's never done that before."

"Never know what a horse is apt to do until you ask it," Slocum said.

"Where to, boss?" Stumpy asked.

"Home to your wife," Slocum said, and shoved Stumpy off the seat. Stumpy fell to the hard street and bounced a couple of times. Slocum looked back to see that Stumpy was more or less okay. He was.

"Good luck, lad," Slocum heard Stumpy cry out. "Try and get me carriage back in one piece."

Slocum whipped the reins to the right; the horses obeyed. They careened onto a street called the Bowery. Up ahead was Steppe's wagon. Slocum grabbed the whip and slapped the horse's rump, spurring it faster. It galloped mightily, and started gaining on Steppe.

No sooner was the wagon in view when Steppe and one of his henchmen started firing at Slocum. He held the reins with one hand and returned the fire with his other. One of the henchmen grabbed his stomach, tumbled from the wagon, and was trampled by Stumpy's horse and cab.

Steppe's wagon careened around a corner. Slocum was right behind him. Steppe grabbed the bolts of expensive Oriental silks from the wagon bed and heaved them at Slocum. One bolt of silk the size of a bedsheet flew into the horse's face, blinding him. Slocum managed to yank it away and snapped the reins, but he was a second too late. The horse started to panic, then ran wild. The right wheel of the buggy jumped into a pothole, overturned and sent Slocum flying.

"Shit," he managed to gasp as he sailed through the air and landed on a pushcart full of half-rotten fruit and vegetables being pushed along the curb by a swarthy Italian man. Oranges, apples, cantaloupes, and artichokes splattered all over the Bowery.

Slocum slid off the pushcart onto the street, covered in crushed produce. Dazed, he lay in the gutter, wondering if any bones were broken. The little Italian angrily jabbed his finger at him, blabbering a string of curses in his native tongue. Just as suddenly the Italian was gone. In his place stood Steppe, accompanied by one of his goons, who had a gun pointed at Slocum's head.

Slocum looked up at Steppe, who grinned with the confidence of a man holding four aces.

"Kill him," Steppe said to his helper, reaching down for an undamaged apple and taking a hefty bite out of it. He tossed the remainder of the apple over his shoulder and walked away.

Slocum looked up into the goon's face. He smiled as he cocked the gun directly at Slocum's head.

Slocum squeezed his eyes shut and waited for the inevitable bullet in his brain.

One shot was fired.

Next station stop, Saint Peter.

There was no pain. He opened his eyes. The goon was sprawled in the gutter, one hand still clutching his unfired gun, deader than the residents of Boot Hill. Blood oozed from a hole in his gullet.

"Good shooting, Bennie," Slocum heard someone behind him say.

Slocum looked up and saw a half dozen men—young, not much more than twenty or twenty-one at the most— wearing derbys and black turtleneck sweaters approach him. Their leader, taller than the others with a hawk-like face consisting of nothing but right angles, said, "You John Slocum?"

"What's left of me," Slocum said. "You plannin' on finishin' off the rest?"

"And why would we want to do that?" asked the leader.

"Everyone else in this town's tried to kill me, so I don't imagine you're any different," Slocum said.

The leader smiled grimly and extended his hand.

"Get up," he said.

Slocum accepted the hand and let the tall man help him up. He rose a bit unsteadily, still reeling from the fall and the latest in the series of close brushes with death.

"I'm obliged to you," Slocum said, dusting himself off. "Would I be out of line if I asked why you decided to save my bacon?"

"We're allowed to save your bacon," the tall man said. "We're just not allowed to eat it."

The other men started laughing. Slocum looked at them quizzically.

"We're the Rivington Street Boys," the tall man said. "The toughest Jewish gang in New York City."

Somehow, the name Rivington Street sounded strangely familiar to Slocum.

"Midnight Rose asked us to keep an eye on you," the tall man said. "Understand you're a friend of hers."

"You could say that," Slocum said.

"I'm David Liebowitz, her cousin," the tall man said. He jerked his head toward the shooter. "This is Dopey Bennie Polakoff, a good man with a gun."

"So I noticed," Slocum said, nodding at Dopey Bennie. "I owe you, Mister Polakoff."

"Was nothing," Dopey Bennie said.

"Let me tell you, Slocum—keeping tabs on you these last few days hasn't been easy," Liebowitz said.

"You sayin' you and your buddies've been trailing me since I got here?" Slocum asked incredulously.

"Trying to," Liebowitz said. "Thought we lost you for sure after your visit to Magpie Maggie's. How do you guys say it in the West? You leave a lot of cold trails, Slocum."

Liebowitz turned away and rejoined his friends, who all started walking away. Liebowitz turned back to Slocum and said, "You coming, cowboy?"

"I got to find Steppe," Slocum replied. "Before *his* trail gets cold."

"He's already vanished into one of his ratholes," Liebowitz said, "and in one hour every gangbanger and crooked cop will be hunting you down. You won't make it a block north of Houston Street." He pronounced it *Howstin*. "You want Steppe, you'll need us. You better come now."

Slocum debated for a moment, then said tiredly, "Ah, what the hell. Worst you can do is kill me."

"From what I've seen, you don't need any help," Liebowitz said.

Slocum stepped off the curb and didn't notice the squashed banana peel lying in wait for his right heel.

He stepped on the banana peel dead-on. His right leg jackknifed, sending him three feet off the ground to land solidly on his backside with a grunt.

Wincing with pain, Slocum reached over and picked up the peel, frowning at it with disgust. The Rivington Street Boys were laughing at him now.

"Know where a man can get a *schnapps* around here?" Slocum asked tiredly, recalling Midnight Rose's word for whiskey.

• • •

Slocum had his drink. Not whiskey, though, but wine. Sweet red wine.

The wine was followed by a seven-course Jewish dinner, starting with a thick chicken broth loaded with delectable dumplings Mrs. Liebowitz called *kreplach*. After this came a roasted chicken with mashed potatoes; some kind of dark noodle product shaped like pellets the old lady called *farfel;* an entire breast of veal, boiled carrots, plates of sour pickles, and light, puffy bread called *challah,* the likes of which Slocum had never tasted.

All of this was prepared by David Liebowitz's sweet-faced, gray-haired mother in the ramshackle kitchen of their Hester Street flat.

"Some more chicken, Mister Slocum?" asked Molly Liebowitz, offering him the platter. She had a middle European accent thicker than Tennessee top soil.

"No thank you, ma'am," Slocum said, stifling a belch. "That *charley* bread just done me in."

"We have lovely fruit compote for dessert and some nice cherry cheesecake," Mrs. Liebowitz said. "You want?"

"Afraid I just ain't got the room after that delicious meal, Mrs. Liebowitz," Slocum said.

David poured Slocum more wine and said to his mother, "Give him the cheesecake. Cousin Rosie said he better not be any skinnier when he comes back than when he left."

David had eaten little; he'd mostly sipped wine and smoked one cigarette after another. His face was pale and drawn, and he seemed preoccupied.

"Just the two of you here?" Slocum asked, taking a sip of wine.

"Just my little *boychik* and me," said Mrs. Liebowitz, smiling at her son as she placed a bowl of fruit swimming in a thick syrup on the table.

"There were some brothers," David said, "but they didn't make it as long as I did. This neighborhood's rough on babies. Fathers, too, who work fifteen hours a day selling rags and bottles." There was bitterness behind every word.

"I understand," Slocum said. "My father dropped dead pushin' a plow over land that yielded rocks and not much else."

"How's my little Rose?" Mrs. Liebowitz asked. "It's been so many years since my *meshuggah* brother-in-law took her away." She turned to her son. "Where is it that Rosie lives?"

"Colorado," David said. "A village called Brushwood Gulch."

Mrs. Liebowitz nodded as though comprehending, but Slocum guessed that her world began and ended both right downstairs on Hester Street.

"Is she eating enough?" Mrs. Liebowitz asked Slocum.

"She's doing just fine," Slocum said, and finally understood David's nervousness. Mrs. Liebowitz was obviously unaware of her niece's chosen profession. "She's a seamstress," he added, "and she's engaged to marry a nice Jewish man who runs the dry goods store."

Slocum saw David relax, then Mrs. Liebowitz said, "Davie said she worked in a hotel."

"She does, she does," Slocum stammered, choking on his wine. "She's a seamstress . . . in the hotel."

"A seamstress in a hotel," Mrs. Liebowitz said, clucking her tongue and walking back into the kitchen. "Only in America . . ."

When she was out of earshot, David smiled at Slocum and said, "Thanks. Mama would wither and die if she knew Rosie was running a whorehouse."

"She's a fine lady regardless," Slocum said.

"You in love with her?"

"Might be," Slocum said.

"She sends us *gelt* every month," David said. "That's money. Don't know how we'd live without her help."

"It's nice that Jewish people stick together," Slocum said.

"Here, we have no choice," David said. "That's why our people need the Rivington Street Boys, when Penderblast sends his army of hooligans down here to beat and rob the Jewish pushcart owners and rag pickers for the few miserable pennies they earn each day."

David rolled himself another cigarette, and Slocum noticed for the first time that he was missing a joint from his middle right finger.

"How'd you lose the finger?" Slocum asked.

"I was one of the ragpickers," David said, and tossed the sack of tobacco to Slocum, who also rolled a cigarette. "Two of Penderblast's goons held me down and cut off my finger because I wouldn't give them my money. They said it was to teach me a lesson. Then they beat my father to death when he tried to help. A tired, skinny old man who wouldn't hurt a fly. Your friend Steppe was one of them. I'm pleased to know he's gone on to bigger things."

David took a few puffs of his cigarette, then said, "If it's all the same to you, Mr. Slocum, I'd like to help you kill the dirty rat."

"Not that I blame you," Slocum replied, "but it ain't killing the man I aim to do."

"Yes, I know," David said. "Mr. Fancy-pants from Colorado still believes in the law. In New York, the law is nothing but a bunch of old yellow newspapers worth less than the orange wrappers we wipe our asses with."

"Don't you worry," Slocum said. "He'll get a trial all right, but you have my solemn word that the jury will find him guilty. When all is said and done, we can both dance on his grave."

There was a loud rap on the warped tenement door. David rose and opened it. A member of the Rivington Street Boys stood in the hallway. Slocum recognized him as his savior, Dopey Bennie.

Dopey Bennie whispered into David's ear and disappeared into the darkness of the cavernous hallway. David turned back to Slocum.

"They know you're here," he said.

"Who knows I'm here?"

"Penderblast and his boys," David said, "and that means the police know you're here, the bastards. It's not safe. We have to take you somewhere else."

"John Slocum never ran from a fight in his life," Slocum said, standing and checking his gun.

"You'll win the fight later," David said, and propelled Slocum out into the hallway. "For now, keeping you alive is the order of the day."

"But your mother," Slocum said, barely grabbing his hat. "I didn't thank her for the dinner."

"If God wills it, you won't get heartburn," David said, slamming his hat on his head and prodding Slocum down the stairs. "For that you can say thanks."

Down on the street, a dozen of the Rivington Street Boys were poised and ready. They all looked grim, nervously clutching their various weapons. With this, Slocum realized the seriousness of the situation: the entire city of New York, it seemed, wanted him either dead or worse.

"Dressed like that," Dopey Bennie said, "he stands out like a pickle in a herring barrel."

There were murmurs of agreement from the rest of the Rivington Street Boys. Slocum found himself being hustled down the street and into the corner tailor shop.

Three minutes later he emerged, the Rivington Street Boys flanking him, dressed like a rabbi, complete with a long black coat, a white prayer shawl David called a *tallith* and a black skullcap called a *yarmelke* planted firmly atop his head. Moe the tailor had also fitted Slocum with a phony black beard. Disguises, David told him, were part of Moe's stock in trade.

"I don't know how to be Jewish," Slocum said as he was quickly escorted through a series of dark, tenement-lined streets.

"Just nod your head and act like you're suffering," David responded.

They arrived at a crumbling tenement and went up some stairs to a dark, shabby flat that was furnished with only a rotting mattress atop a rusted bed and a couple of uncomfortable wooden chairs.

"You'll be safe here," David told him.

"Can I have my clothes back?" Slocum asked. "Nothing personal, but a man can't rightly hold his head up dressed like a rabie."

"That's *rabbi*," David said. "I think maybe my boys and me will hold on to them so you can't get into any trouble."

"Then how about my gun?" he asked.

"That you can have, but only if you promise to stay here until we say it's safe for you to leave."

"You've done right by me so far," Slocum said. "Reckon it wouldn't be right courteous for me to skedaddle."

"*Mazel tov*, paleface," David said, throwing Slocum's holster on the bed. "You answered correctly."

Slocum watched as the Rivington Street Boys filed out of the flat. David was the last one out.

"We'll be back tomorrow sometime." He tossed Slocum his pouch of tobacco. "High noon is good?"

"Perfect," Slocum said, and rolled himself a smoke.

15

It was a long night.

At midnight or thereabouts, Slocum was driven out of bed by voracious bedbugs and red ants that marched out of the rotting wooden floor to devour him. At one in the morning, Slocum had placed each leg of the bed into four rusty chamberpots filled with ammonia from a bottle he found under the filthy sink down the hall. The ants were halted, leaving Slocum to the mercy of the bedbugs. At three A.M., Slocum sought refuge on the rusting fire escape, where he managed to get a few minutes' sleep until the first rays of the morning sun brought a gaggle of weary tenement housewives out to hang laundry.

One of them, a stooped-over old gal with gray hair, stopped and waved at Slocum, her mouth crammed full of clothespins.

"Top of the mornin' to you, Rabbi," she hollered across the alley.

Slocum was at first puzzled, then remembered his new attire.

"Good *mazel tov,* to you, ma'am," Slocum said, waving back and tipping the black hat Moe the tailor had given him. For good measure, he also tipped the *yarmelke* he was wearing under it.

Slocum heard someone pounding on the door. He scrambled through the window and drew his gun from the holster strapped around the long black rabbi's frock coat. Leaning against the wall adjacent to the door, he yelled, "State your business."

"You're my business," he heard a familiar female voice say.

Slocum grabbed the doorknob and said, "How do I know you're alone?"

"You don't," he heard Sally Balls call back. "You're just gonna have to trust me."

Slocum unlocked the door, then crouched back away from it.

"I don't trust anyone in this town," he said. "Come in with your hands touching the sky."

The door opened slowly. Slocum watched as Sally Balls walked in slowly, then kicked the door shut.

"Cut the crap, Slocum," she called out, not yet seeing him. "I'm alone and unarmed."

"You're also very pretty," Slocum said from behind her. And she was, clad in the prettiest pink dress Slocum had ever seen, though an inch or two above the ankle for what barely passed as respectable.

She spun and looked at him skeptically, not at all fazed by his new wardrobe.

"Very nice," Sally Balls said, the sarcasm in her tone hard to miss. "The gentile Kid rides again."

Slocum holstered the gun. "Do you want to insult me or do you want to tell me why you're here?"

"I'd like to do both but we ain't got the time," she said.

"What do you want?" Slocum asked.

"You played me for a sucker, you dirty prick," she said, grabbing a chair and daintily sitting. "Made me mad enough so's I'd tell you about the robbery."

"I'm here for a reason," Slocum said. "What did you expect me to do? If your feelings got in the way, my apologies."

She sprang up, fury etched in her pretty face, and said, "Apology not accepted."

She walked up to Slocum and threw her arms around him. "It's not an apology I want, Slocum," she said softly. "It's your lips on mine that I'd prefer."

She grabbed the lapels of Slocum's coat and pulled him close, then planted her lips on his. Slocum found himself circling his arms tightly around her waist, kissing her back. Sally Balls rubbed her body against his, and within seconds his manhood started standing at attention.

At about the same time Slocum attempted to cup her tight buttocks in his hands, Sally Balls slid her hand down Slocum's back and, reaching under the long coat, grabbed his testicles. She gave them a healthy squeeze, clutching them tightly.

Slocum heard himself squeal in pain. He pushed her away, so that she landed flat on the bed.

"I know you're mad," Slocum said, massaging his crotch, "but that's no reason to make me a gelding."

Sally Balls lay seductively on the bed and started unbuttoning her blouse.

"Feeling warm?" Slocum asked.

"You might say that," Sally Balls said.

She disrobed slowly, revealing a pair of breasts so firm, so perfect that Slocum had to struggle to keep from drooling. She seductively cupped them in her hands.

"Don't you think you're pushing the boundaries of good taste here?" Slocum's gaze held firmly to her naked chest.

"That look on your mug tells me you'd like to push them a little further," she said.

There were a million reasons not to, of course, not the least of which was incurring the wrath of Liebowitz for two-timing his cousin. In the end, though, Slocum knew he'd turn to the solace of his favorite expression: A stiff pecker has no conscience.

Slocum walked to the bed, throwing off clothes along the way. Sally Balls anxiously squirmed out of her dress and bloomers.

"I don't do this with everyone I meet, you understand," Sally Balls said as Slocum slid on top of her. "Just the people I like."

Slocum saw no advantage of arguing the point and immediately got down to business. He kissed her hard, gliding his tongue into her mouth. Sally Balls wrapped her legs around his waist and held him tightly, guiding his member into her.

Slocum prodded her furry mound with the tip of his pulsing member. Sally Balls groaned in anticipation.

"Put it in me," she begged.

Slocum prodded her moist lovenest again, penetrating her an inch or so, then withdrawing.

"For Chrissakes," Sally Balls panted, her breathing fast and hard. "Love me, Slocum."

Still he toyed with her, tantalizing her with the tip of his shaft. Sally Balls sank her sharp fingernails into the flesh of his back.

"What are you waiting for?" she asked, wanting him badly.

"Where's Steppe?" he asked.

"You never give up, do you?" she said, and grabbed his buttocks. She forced him deeply into her, wrapping herself around him like a slab of bacon on a stick.

Their bodies bucked in perfect rhythm, arms and legs intertwined. Slocum had never known such pleasure—at least since his last session with Midnight Rose. As he thrust his hips at her—and Sally Balls thrust hers upwards to meet him—he knew that holding back would be tougher than year-old jerky.

"Tell me," Slocum gasped, pumping her mercilessly.

"Love me now," she gasped. "Talk later."

Slocum buried his face in her shapely neck and did as he was told. Soon Sally Balls was crying out in ecstasy, gripping him even tighter.

"Oh, ride 'em, cowboy," she squealed delightedly.

His passion mounted, matched only by hers, and they climaxed, their bodies locked in a sweaty embrace. Sally Balls let out a little animal-like yelp, biting his ear and sinking her nails deeper into his back. These New York gals made love the way they lived—tough and hard.

They relaxed now, their breathing a little slower. Slocum made no effort to roll off of her, rather enjoying the post-love glow.

"You didn't answer my question," Slocum whispered in her ear, and nibbled on her neck.

Sally Balls pushed him away and got up off the bed. She grabbed her clothes and started getting dressed.

"I wanted you the minute I saw you, Slocum," she said, buttoning her blouse. "Right there in the river, your baby blues begging me to save your skin. I could see behind those eyes was a good heart."

"Waterlogged as it was," Slocum said. "Why did you come back?"

"I wanted to see you one last time before you left," she said. "You're going home today."

"Says who?" Slocum wanted to know, putting on his rabbi clothes.

"The people who brought you here most likely," she said. "The Rivington Street Boys. They also have a score to settle and it's my guess they want you out of the game."

"We'll see about that," Slocum muttered, feeling truly ridiculous now in the long black coat and hat.

"Better put the beard on," she suggested. "Don't want to go out of here half dressed."

"Very funny," Slocum said, strapping on his gun. "Come on, I'll walk you downstairs to the street."

"Such a gentlemen," Sally Balls said, and together they went out the door and started down the winding stair-case.

"How did you find me here, by the way?" Slocum said.

"I have my ways," was all she said.

They walked down the long, dark tenement hallway toward the door to the street, with Sally Balls in the lead. In the foyer she stopped and turned to him.

"Well, it's been fun, Slocum," she said, kissing him on the cheek. "Too bad you have to go. I think we could have had something special."

"You never know what kind of hand fate's going to deal you," Slocum said.

"Got a sweetie back home?"

"Maybe."

They turned and walked out onto the street. Several shots rang out, and Slocum ducked instinctively. From the corner of his eye he saw Sally Balls clutch her belly, a huge red blotch spreading fast. She crumpled to the sidewalk.

All over the street, dozens of innocent bystanders scrambled for safety as more shots rang out. Slocum rolled to the left and sprinted behind a metal dustbin, gun drawn. The shots seemed to be coming from an alleyway across the street between two tenements.

Slocum peered out from behind the bin. He saw the shadowy forms of two people—most definitely his assailants—pressed flat against the brick tenement. Another shot rang out, hitting the cobblestone six inches away. Slocum decided there was enough of the gunner visible now to make his move pay off, though it would mean exposing himself. Not that he had any choice—his attackers had him pinned down good.

Slocum leaped up and, aiming for the shadows, squeezed off three shots. He heard a cry of pain, then, peering from behind the dustbin, he saw someone fall into the garbage-strewn alleyway.

The other shadow was gone, most likely running down the alleyway to the next block. Slocum made his way back to where Sally Balls was lying, a pool of blood on the sidewalk next to her.

Slocum cradled her in his arms. Her face was ashen, her hands ice-cold.

"Hold on, Sally," Slocum whispered as curious onlookers began to cluster around them. "We'll get you to a doc."

"I'm heading for the last roundup, Slocum," Sally Balls said weakly. "You want Steppe, you'll find him tonight at Clancy's Saloon on Water Street. Plays a high-stakes poker game every Tuesday no matter what. But don't go it alone, Slocum . . ." She coughed up blood. "If you're crazy enough to try, get his two bodyguards first, Pickles Mayhew and Goo Goo Knox. They're tough *hombres* . . . but I think you're tougher."

Her eyelids fluttered. "Take care, Slocum," she said, her voice barely a whisper. "Remember . . . the streets giveth and the streets taketh away."

Her body went limp in his arms.

Slocum released her lifeless body and started reloading his gun. "Where does that alleyway across the street go?" he asked a withered old man clutching a broom.

"Don't go nowheres," the man said.

"I was hopin' you'd say that," Slocum said, madder than hell but still in control, though barely. He rose and cautiously approached the entrance of the alley, saw one of the gunmen lying facedown, not moving. Slocum slid the toe of his boot under the man and rolled him over. A huge chunk of his face had been shot away.

Slocum crouched against the wall and cautiously made his way down the alley. Across the way, the warped wooden door to a shabby tenement flapped open and shut in the breeze, the rusty hinges creaking. Someone had just gone through that door, Slocum knew, since there didn't appear to be any other way out of the alley.

He pulled the door open with his boot and peered inside. It was darker than midnight in there, the weak oil lamps barely throwing off more than a futile glow along the hallway, which led to a flight of stairs. Again, Slocum pressed himself against the wall and inched his way toward the stairs. The hallway smelled of urine and long ago dinners of cabbage. He could hear dogs barking, babies crying, and people screaming in languages Slocum had never heard before.

He approached the stairs and started climbing them slowly, kicking cans and bottles out of the way.

"Damn people live like pigs," he muttered.

Slocum was maybe five steps from the second floor landing when a large figure moved like lightning from

the gloom and fired directly at him. Slocum had the good
sense to duck and came up shooting, though by this time
the shooter had blended back into the darkness.

Slocum heard someone running up the stairs above him.
He decided to follow, bounding up the steps two at a time
until he reached the top landing, and heard the door to
the roof being pushed open. Sunlight flooded onto the top
floor landing.

Slocum stepped out onto the roof and saw chickens and
pigeons in coops; there were even a couple of piglets
penned up and squealing excitedly.

A shot rang out from behind one of the chicken coops
and smashed into the roof door behind him. Slocum dived
for cover as chickens cackled and pigeons fluttered against
the confines of their cages.

"Don't be shootin' our damned dinner," Slocum heard
someone cry out in an apartment below.

Slocum crouched behind the open door and attempted
to return the fire. His prey suddenly ran out from behind
the chicken coop, firing twice in Slocum's direction and,
to Slocum's amazement, jumped off the edge of the roof
and onto the roof of a tenement across the alley, a good ten
feet at least. The gunner barely faltered and kept running
across the rooftop.

Slocum, not thinking twice, did the same. He got a
running start, ran to the edge of the roof, let out a war
whoop, and jumped. He began to sail effortlessly over the
open space between the buildings. Halfway across though,
he saw Sally's killer step out from behind a chimney and
fire at him.

It was none other than her partner-in-crime, Ugly
Mabel.

Slocum lost his momentum and knew he'd fall short of
the rooftop. He was right. He managed to grab onto the

two-foot-high brick wall that lined the tenement roof and held on for dear life. It was a straight drop down to the street of at least a hundred feet.

Mabel loomed above him, grinning from ear to ear. She pointed the barrel of the gun at Slocum's head.

"I swore I'd kill you one day," she said. "And that day is now."

"You wouldn't shoot a rabbi, would you?" Slocum asked, dangling helplessly.

"No, but I'd stomp him," she said, and smashed her foot down on his hand, though not his shooting one. He felt a couple of knuckles snap followed by a red-hot pain that shot all the way down his arm.

Mabel raised her other foot to smash his good hand, but before she could bring it down a shot rang out behind him. Slocum saw Mabel weave from side to side, almost dreamily. Blood spurted from a hole in her heart, then she pitched forward and over the side of the building. Slocum watched her fall the hundred feet and land with a sickening thud into a pile of rotting lumber.

Slocum twisted his head and ventured a look at the opposite rooftop.

"Now we're even, you bastard," Flannery said, and blew the smoke of the barrel of his gun.

"Pretty good shooting for a New Yorker," Slocum said.

16

Slocum sat on a hard wooden bench in the middle of Grand Central Station, flanked on either side by two burly policemen. Flannery had taken the liberty of handcuffing Slocum to one of the policemen, a bearded bear of a man named Muldoon. The train to Chicago was set to depart in fifteen minutes, and Flannery intended to place Slocum on board personally.

Flannery paced impatiently back and forth, pausing every now and then to glare at Slocum. Slocum hadn't noticed at first when Flannery shot Ugly Mabel off the roof, that both of his eyes were blackened now. It was comical in a way, though Flannery saw little humor in it, especially after his precinct captain, McPhee, had questioned him on the two black eyes. Knowing that Captain McPhee wouldn't buy anything but the truth, Flannery told him just that.

To which Captain McPhee had replied, "You're getting old, Kevin Flannery. Weren't too many could get the drop on you, time was."

McPhee wanted to meet this Slocum, who'd managed

singlehandedly to turn New York upside down. The newspapers had gotten wind of his exploits and made them front page news. "Gunfight on OK Canal Street," blared the headline in the *Herald Examiner,* while the *New York Tribune* trumpeted, "High Noon in Lower Manhattan: Colorado Sheriff Comes Gunning For Justice." Within twenty-four hours of the shootout at the warehouse, the people of New York were enamored with "Big John Slocum," as the papers coined him.

After the rooftop incident, Flannery spirited Slocum— who was still dressed like a rabbi—back uptown to the precinct. They were greeted by dozens of journalists, all clamoring for interviews with Slocum.

"Keep your mouth shut," Flannery hissed at Slocum as the reporters closed in on them. "We'll all be better off."

Slocum was hustled into McPhee's office. McPhee looked to be nearing sixty, though he could have been younger. The residents of New York, Slocum had noted, seemed old before their time.

Slocum sat in a chair, with Flannery standing behind him. McPhee, ruddy-faced and jowly from what looked like years of sucking up hooch, smiled condescendingly at Slocum. He was holding a newspaper. He adjusted his bifocals and read, " 'In a city where you can fire a gun in any direction without hitting an honest man, it's refreshing to see a brave and true individual such as Sheriff John Slocum. He came to New York seeking justice and doled out some of his own, the kind of justice that is fast, hard, and permanent.' "

McPhee eyed Slocum sharply and continued.

" 'Like a tornado sweeping through the grain fields of Kansas, Big John Slocum has singlehandedly smashed through the shadowy dark walls of New York's underworld with nothing but a six-shooter and a gallon of raw guts and courage. In less than a week, Sheriff Slocum has wreaked more havoc on the criminal element than the entire Metropolitan Police Force has been able to, their principal concerns being the prevention of such heinous crimes as public intoxication, maltreatment of animals, interference of telegraph wires, and the conducting of dogfights, cockfights, prizefights, as well as theatrical entertainments on Sunday.' "

McPhee slammed the paper down and leaned on his desk, hands pressed flat on the surface.

"Just who the hell do you think you are, Slocum?" McPhee snapped. "Come to my city and make a ruckus, will you? Take the law into your own hands, will you? Just answer me this, Mr. Big John: If I were to come to your town in Colorado—not that I'd be caught dead any further west than Tenth Avenue—and tried to dole out my own brand of Eastern justice, and—"

"And if the boot was on the other foot?" Slocum said. "I'd most likely try to help you."

"I don't need your help, Slocum," McPhee said. "Not here nor anywhere. And I don't suffer vigilantes gladly." He looked at Flannery. "What time is the next train west out of Grand Central Station?"

"Two hours," Flannery said.

"I want him on it," McPhee said. "Chained to the back of the caboose if necessary." He looked at Slocum and continued, "The more the newspapers glorify you, Slocum, the more people will start taking the law into their own hands, and that's something I can't afford. You've made your point, now you're going home."

Whereupon Slocum was escorted to Grand Central Station by Flannery and the two big Irish cops in the paddy wagon. Inside was a change of clothes—Levis, blue denim shirt, and even a ten-gallon hat a size too small. On the ride to Grand Central, Slocum shed his rabbi attire and slipped into his new duds. Flannery handed him a receipt from the clothing store where the clothes were bought.

"I expect Brushwood Gulch to reimburse the city of New York for your new outfit," Flannery said dryly.

"We're good for it," Slocum said, snatching the receipt from Flannery. When he finished dressing, Flannery slapped handcuffs on him, binding his wrists.

"Are these really necessary?" Slocum asked.

"Yes, and they don't come off until you get to Chicago," Flannery said. "And to see that you do, Officer Muldoon has graciously agreed to accompany you there."

Muldoon grinned at him, six feet and six inches tall, a side of beef in a uniform.

"Does he eat real food or does he need to graze?" Slocum asked, regarding the brawny dick.

Upon their arrival at Grand Central, Slocum was handcuffed to Muldoon for safekeeping.

When the other cop, O'Donnell, opened the door to the paddy wagon, they were greeted by a horde of newspaper and magazine journalists, exploding powder, and the blinding flashes of photographers' cameras. As they jumped down off the back of the wagon, the crowd swarmed around Slocum, pencils and paper in their hands.

"Going home, Sheriff Slocum?" one newspaperman asked.

"Kind of looks that way," he replied. Flannery glared at him, showing teeth.

Flannery motioned to Muldoon and O'Donnell, who grabbed Slocum's right arm, while Muldoon merely yanked the handcuffs. They half dragged Slocum through the crowd. Undeterred, the eager journalists followed and the questions flew.

"Get your man, Slocum?"

"Not yet," Slocum said.

"Word has it, Slocum, that you're going after the big man himself, Boss Penderblast," said another reporter.

"I got no argument with any Boss Penderblast," Slocum said, and Muldoon jerked him harder. "It's one of his employees I'm looking for, Samuel St—"

O'Donnell whacked Slocum in the knee with his billy club. Slocum went down, taking Muldoon with him. They crumpled into a heap ten feet from the entrance of Grand Central Station.

Flannery went down on one knee and started to help Slocum up, then whispered in his ear, "You'd best be keepin' your mouth shut, pard."

He helped Slocum to his feet.

"How many men have you killed, Sheriff?" asked a reporter.

"Only them that needed killing," he replied.

"Do you know Jesse James? Billy the Kid?"

"No, but I met Magpie Maggie and Razor Riley," Slocum said.

"Ever ride with the Dalton Gang?" asked another reporter.

"No, but I rode with Stumpy Marlarkey," he said.

Slocum played the rest of the reporters' questions close to the vest until they were inside the train station, where a dozen more policemen were ready to hold back the adoring press.

"Okay, the interview's over," Flannery said to the crowd. "Sheriff Slocum is homesick for Colorado and is eager to get home. Now if you'll excuse us . . ."

"If he's so eager," cracked one reporter, Jake Davis from the *Brooklyn Eagle,* "how come you got the cuffs on him?"

"The handcuffs are for protection," Flannery said.

"Slocum's protection?" Davis asked.

"No, ours."

The squad of cops made the newspaper people disperse. Flannery plunked Slocum and Muldoon onto a bench; O'Donnell took a seat on Slocum's left. Slocum felt like the filling in a cop sandwich.

Flannery took to pacing back and forth, checking his pocket watch every two minutes.

"Forty-two minutes and you'll be out of my life forever," Flannery said, putting the watch away in a vest pocket. "Don't get me wrong, Slocum, I think under the right circumstances we could have been drinking buddies."

"I guess," Slocum said, "to know me is to love me."

"Not to know you is to love you more," Flannery said. "Do yourself a favor, Slocum, and don't come back to this city. If you do, we'll be forced to hunt you down and kill you, and quite frankly, I would hate to see that happen. You're a good man, though somewhat misguided."

Flannery continued pacing and checked his watch again.

"Forty-one minutes," he said.

Slocum took a look around the station to relieve the boredom of waiting. Maybe they'd get him as far as Chicago, he thought, but he'd be on the first train back.

Slocum took note of a man standing next to the men's room, his face hidden by what Slocum recognized as a Hebrew-language newspaper. Slocum recalled seeing signs in that same language during his brief visit to the lower East Side.

A face appeared over the top of the newspaper. It belonged to David Liebowitz. Davie winked at Slocum, who also noticed the ever-reliable Dopey Bennie Polakoff stroll up as well. Davie pointed to the men's room sign, then went back to his newspaper.

"I got to drain my cactus," Slocum said to Flannery.

"Drain it when you get on the train," Flannery replied.

"It ain't for more than a half hour," Slocum said. "Come on, Flannery, you know how it feels. Unless you traded your pecker for that badge."

Rather than get angry, Flannery just looked exasperated. "All right, Slocum," he said, sounding tired.

Slocum attempted to stand but only got halfway up, forgetting momentarily he was still cuffed to Muldoon.

"Go with him, Muldoon," Flannery said.

Muldoon complied, the tall cop getting up and taking long strides toward the men's room, half dragging Slocum in the process. They walked right by Davie and Dopey Bennie, who was down on one knee, pretending to shine Davie's shoe with the rolled-up newspaper.

The bathroom, Slocum saw, was quite impressive. There was a barber shop, a shoe-shine stand, and a white-uniformed Negro attendant handing out towels and dispensing after-shave.

Muldoon stopped in the middle of the room and said to Slocum, "Go ahead and be quick about it."

Slocum saw that they were standing a good ten or so feet from the urinals.

"I'm good, Muldoon," Slocum said, "but I can't pee that far."

"Oh, yeah," Muldoon said, the idea finally making an impression inside his thick skull.

Muldoon grunted and walked Slocum over to the urinal. Knowing he had to buy some time, Slocum unzipped his fly and started to relieve himself. Muldoon seemed oblivious to the fact that Davie and Dopey Bennie were creeping up behind him. Dopey Bennie produced a blackjack and smashed it down on Muldoon's skull.

Muldoon barely flinched. He turned his head and looked at Dopey Bennie.

"Why did you do that?" Muldoon asked, not so much mad but confused.

Dopey Bennie shrugged and hit Muldoon again, twice as hard this time. The second blow managed to do some damage, but not quite enough. Muldoon spun around, dragging the still-urinating Slocum with him. Muldoon grabbed Dopey Bennie by the lapels and flung him across the length of the men's room. Before he could shut off his bladder, Slocum squirted a stream of piss straight up in the air that rained down squarely on Muldoon's head.

Davie Liebowitz jumped onto Muldoon's back and locked his arms around the copper's bull neck. Muldoon struggled to throw Davie off, but he held tight. They danced around in a circle, dragging Slocum along. His exposed member took the opportunity to dig itself painfully into his zipper. Slocum suppressed the howl of agony he knew would alert Flannery and every cop within earshot.

Dopey Bennie scrambled to his feet and dived into the fray, tackling Muldoon around the ankles. It was like trying to bring down a runaway streetcar. All four of them tumbled to the floor. The shoe-shine man and attendant huddled inside a toilet stall, peering out occasionally to watch the action.

"Dat man got hisself stuck bad," the shoe-shine man said, seeing Slocum's prickly predicament.

"Don't y'all look at me," replied the attendant, who was crouched down beside the shoe-shine man, also watching the action. "I ain't gonna help him, no suh. Dey his balls, dey his problem."

"Amen, brother," said the shoe-shine man.

For no other reason than to stop Muldoon from thrashing around so he could extricate his manhood from his zipper, Slocum grabbed Muldoon's billy club. It took three solid wallops before it cracked in half and Muldoon stopped struggling.

"Oh God, oh God," Slocum muttered, managing to free himself from the agonizing clutches of his zipper. "Nice work, boys," he added, "but next time, please wait until I'm done pissing."

"Where's the key to the cuffs?" Davie asked, frantically going through Muldoon's pockets.

"You're wasting your time," Slocum said, gingerly zipping himself up. "Flannery's got it."

"That could be a problem," Davie said.

17

Davie, Dopey Bennie, and Slocum hoisted the unconscious Muldoon to his feet, no simple task. Slocum and
Dopey Bennie supported him while Davie threw his coat
over Muldoon's shoulders. He grabbed Dopey Bennie's
battered derby and jammed it onto Muldoon's head. It
was at least four sizes too small, but it would do for the
time being.

Davie went to the shoe-shine man's box and grabbed
some black shoe polish. He dipped his pinky into it and
proceeded to skillfully paint a moustache on Muldoon's
upper lip.

"Let's go, Rembrandt," Dopey Bennie barked.

They marched, three abreast, to the door of the
men's room, Slocum and Dopey Bennie supporting the
coldcocked cop. Davie, in the lead, opened the door to
check for the bulls. Standing there were Flannery and two
of his men, obviously coming to check on the delay.

"Routine three, Bennie," Davie said. Together they
kneed the two startled cops on either side of Flannery

firmly in the groin. Even before New York's finest doubled over and became New York's flattest, Slocum and his friends started running, knocking Flannery aside. Flannery stumbled backwards and crashed into a bench, then tumbled ass backwards over it.

"This way," Davie cried, and they dashed down a corridor, lugging Muldoon's inert body, which seriously hampered their progress. Flannery, flat on his back, pulled out his whistle and blew shrilly on it. Every cop in Grand Central Station came running.

The policemen congregated around Flannery, who was sprawled out on top of two slumbering drunks who had graciously broken his fall.

"You okay, Mr. Flannery?" asked one cop.

Flannery pointed to the corridor where Slocum and his cohorts made their getaway.

"Catch them or you'll all be walking beats in the belly of Brooklyn," he yelled.

A sea of blue uniformed cops cascaded down the corridor, knocking over whoever and whatever was in their path—apple carts, candy hawkers, and passersby alike.

"Down here," Davie snapped, and they turned down another corridor that led to an exit on Lexington Avenue. Before they rounded the corner, Slocum saw the regiment of policemen flooding the corridor behind them, nightsticks raised and ready to crack some heads.

"Let's move it," Slocum cried. They half ran, half dragged Muldoon to the exit door and burst through it. At the same time, Stumpy Malarkey brought his hansom cab to a halt at the curb outside. They went straight for it, hoisting Muldoon and Slocum inside.

"A pleasure to see you again, Mr. Slocum," Stumpy said, tipping his hat.

"The pleasure's all mine," Slocum said as Davie and

Dopey Bennie climbed aboard. "Now let's get the hell out of here."

"I thought you might be saying that," Stumpy said, and snapped his whip at the horse's rump. The cab lurched forward and down the street. "Where to?"

"A locksmith," Davie said, "and I know the best one in town. My cousin Abraham on Hester Street."

"Hester Street it is," Stumpy said, and headed downtown on Lexington Avenue, expertly dodging trolleys and pedestrians.

Cousin Abraham, a tall, gaunt-faced man in his late thirties, hacksawed through the handcuffs that made Slocum and Muldoon unwilling partners. Muldoon was still unconscious, thanks to a few additional blows on the noggin delivered on the ride downtown, when the big cop began showing signs of coming to.

"Good pair of cuffs," Cousin Abraham said, working the saw like a man possessed. "The finest steel money can buy, probably army issue."

"Just get 'em off," Davie said.

Abraham continued sawing. "Don't rush an artist, Davie, when he's working. You want speed, lock him in a safe. I'll have him out in ten seconds." When he wasn't tending to his locksmith business, Abraham Schwartz plied his true trade: safecracking.

"Abie's the best safecracker in New York," Davie said with a tinge of pride. "His services are always in demand."

"No orchids, Davie," Abraham said, making slow progress. They were in the back room of his Hester Street shop. Abe posted the "closed" sign on the door after his cousin Davie and his pals had shown up. Except for a few burning candles, the shop was dark. "Is this your first visit to New York, Mr. Slocum?" Abe asked.

"My last," Slocum said. "Now saw through these cuffs and be quick about it."

"Take it easy, Mr. Fancy-pants Cowboy," Abe said. "I'll get you free quicker than Lincoln freed the slaves."

"Why did you come back for me?" Slocum asked Davie, who was devouring a sandwich of smoked salmon on black bread.

Davie tore off half the sandwich and handed it to Slocum. He wolfed it down.

"I told Rose I'd make sure you got back in one piece," Davie said. "Even if the cops got you out of New York, I knew you would give them the slip and come back, and probably get killed in the process. I'm going to help you get your man, Slocum. It's the only way we'll get you home to Colorado alive."

"Appreciate the offer," Slocum said. "But I can take him by myself. Besides, if you're seen, Penderblast and his boys'll be on you faster than beans on rice."

"I thought maybe a smart sheriff like yourself would want a posse," Davie said. "Your friend is going to have a lot of men protecting him."

"Maybe, maybe not," Slocum said. "By the time he reads the newspapers, he'll know I was given the bum's rush out of town. As far as Steppe's concerned, I'm somewhere in the cornfields of Indiana."

"Unless someone tips him off that you escaped," Davie said. "Penderblast has a lot of police on the payroll."

"Yeah, there is that," Slocum said. "Guess that makes the odds two to one he's ready for me. You know something, Liebowitz? I've faced worse odds since I got here."

Cousin Abraham wiped his sweaty brow with a hanky and continued sawing away.

"How much longer?" Slocum asked him.

"Always in such a rush," Cousin Abraham said, shaking

his head. "So you're taking on one of Penderblast's big boys?"

"You heard right," Slocum said.

"To be perfectly honest, my *meshugah* friend," Cousin Abraham said, "with his two thousand guns against your two, that's not what I call a fair fight. Ah, but that's what I love about America. Every man has the freedom to go out and get himself killed however he wants."

"Stop *kibitzing* already and get those cuffs off," Dopey Bennie said.

Each time Muldoon started groggily coming around, Dopey Bennie sent him back into dreamland with the help of a wooden club.

"Would you hurry," Slocum said.

"Another half inch to his wrist," said Cousin Abraham. "Twenty minutes at the most. What, maybe you don't want to be late for your own funeral? There's an old Jewish proverb, Mr. Slocum: If death is waiting around the corner, take a different street."

"What if there ain't another street?" Slocum asked.

"Then you turn around and walk the other way," Abraham said. "So, have you ever seen a real Indian?"

"I've seen a few and killed a few," Slocum said.

"I'm told they wear paint on their faces and give you a haircut like you never had before with their tommyhawks," he said.

"Something like that," Slocum said.

"Terrible, terrible," Cousin Abraham said, clucking his tongue. "Grown men acting that way. Have you ever eaten a buffalo?"

"My share," Slocum said.

"I hear you can use their poop for fuel," Cousin Abraham said.

"It's kept me from freezing to death a time or two," Slocum said.

"I'm told riding around on a horse all day gives you the piles." Cousin Abraham didn't even flinch as Dopey Bennie clunked Muldoon again.

"That's true," Slocum said, "and as long as we're on the subject of pains in the ass, think you could step up the pace a bit?"

Ten minutes later Abraham sawed clean through the steel around Slocum's wrist without severing any important arteries. Slocum thanked him, and Davie and Dopey Bennie hustled him back into Stumpy's waiting hansom. Davie said to his cousin, "Get some of the boys and dump that cop somewhere on Third Avenue, away from the neighborhood."

Abraham clutched the wooden club Dopey Bennie had given him and said, "Not to worry, it will be a pleasure."

Stumpy got them moving. "Where to?"

"Clancy's Saloon on Water Street," Slocum said. "Wherever that is."

Stumpy said, knowing he'd probably never see his new friend again after tonight, "And don't worry about the money you owe me."

"You're a good man, Malarkey," Slocum said.

"I'll just cash in the train ticket Detective Flannery gave you," Stumpy said, waving it for Slocum to see.

"You'll probably need some decent weapons, so here," Davie said, rummaging through a paper bag Cousin Abraham had given him. He pulled out two Colt revolvers. "God made man, Slocum, but it took the gun to make us all equal." He handed them to Slocum. "*Abi-gezunt,* live and be well."

"Good *gesundheit* to you too," Slocum said. "And thanks. Do yourself a favor and come to Colorado.

It's good country for good people. We could use more like you."

"Maybe I will," Davie said. "It's probably impossible to get a good pickle anywhere in the territory. I'll go into business."

They pulled up in front of a waterfront hellhole bordering the East River. Unlike the west side waterfront, this one was totally deserted, as though these streets were pure evil, where few dared to venture.

"The offer still stands, Slocum," Davie said. "We'll back you."

Slocum surveyed the spooky surroundings and reasoned that a little help probably wouldn't hurt. "Are your chambers filled, boys?" he asked Davie and Dopey Bennie.

"What do we look like, chopped liver?" Dopey Bennie snorted, brandishing a gun. "Let's kill somebody."

"Just wait here," Slocum said, vaulting out of the cab onto the street. "You hear gunfire, enter as your conscience dictates—and at your own risk."

Slocum turned to Stumpy. "Give my best to the missus if I don't come back," he said.

Stumpy shook his head. "Me gut tells me I'll be sharing a glass of bitters with you soon, Slocum. Enough of your silly good-byes. Go do your job."

Slocum tipped an imaginary hat at Stumpy, then turned and walked toward the door of Clancy's Saloon.

"Let's finish it," Slocum said to no one in particular.

18

Slocum pounded on the saloon door, not even sure that Steppe was there. A slot at eye level opened and a man's bulldog face appeared.

"State your business," the man growled.

Slocum grabbed the man's nose in a pincer-like grip and gave it a twist. The man howled in pain and tried to pull his head back, but Slocum held firm.

"Quit your yowling or I'll tear it off completely," Slocum said.

"Whaddaya want?" the man cried through closed nostrils.

"Samuel Steppe," Slocum said. "Is he in there?"

"Go to hell," the man said, and Slocum twisted his bulbous nose again.

"I'll ask you again," Slocum said, clenching the guy's honker like a vise. "Is Samuel Steppe in there?"

"He was, he was," the man stammered, "but he left."

"You're a liar," Slocum said, and gave the guy's nose a hard twist. He could hear bones and cartilage crack. Blood started gushing out onto Slocum's hand. The pain was so excruciating that the man didn't even notice that Slocum had released his grip. In an instant, Slocum had the barrel of his gun resting squarely on the broken bridge of the man's nose.

"Open the door or I swear to God your brains will decorate the wall."

"Okay, mister, whatever you say," the man said. "Just ease off that trigger."

Slocum said, "Let me hear you pull those latches back."

He heard the clinking of latches being pulled. His gun never left the man's face.

"Now open it slowly, like you would for your mother," Slocum said. The door opened half an inch. Slocum pushed his way in and cracked the man over the head with the butt of his gun. Three well placed wallops did the trick. The ape went to the floor, unconscious.

Slocum found himself in a dark, deserted saloon. The tables were overturned and broken chairs were scattered everywhere. No doubt this establishment had seen a nasty brawl recently.

He could hear the sounds of a poker game in full swing in a room at the end of a dark hallway. The door to this room, too, was shut tight. Slocum could see light filtering out from under it.

Before he could move a step, the door opened and a tall man wearing a red undershirt and suspenders came out carrying two big glass pitchers. Slocum dropped to the floor and crawled behind a table that had been tipped over.

"Sweet bloody Jesus, Patsy," the man called out. "Where the hell is that beer? I told you to—"

The man stopped dead, already alert to the fact that something was amiss. He turned to walk back.

"Move an inch and I plug you," Slocum said.

"What do you want?" the man asked nervously.

"Is Samuel Steppe in that room?"

"Samuel Steppe? Never heard of him," the man said.

"Turn around," Slocum said. The man did, slowly, with the practiced moves of a man who had seen his share of trouble.

"Where's Patsy?" the big man said.

"Sleeping one off," Slocum said, peering out from behind the table. The big man, who was standing about six feet away from Slocum, hurled an empty glass pitcher at him. Slocum ducked behind the table as the pitcher shattered against it. Quick as a weasel the man pulled out a dagger and flung it at the spot where Slocum's head had been half a second earlier. He turned and started to run down the hall, dropping the other pitcher.

"He's here, boss," the man called out.

Slocum jumped up and fired at the retreating figure, catching him between the shoulder blades. The guy staggered and bounced off the walls. Before he even had time to fall, another man jumped into the hallway and started blasting, succeeding only in pumping four more shots into his mortally wounded buddy.

The guy dropped like a bag of lead, blood spurting through nearly half a dozen holes in his head and chest. What looked like five or six men streamed out of the room, several carrying rifles. Simultaneously they all belched out a barrage of bullets in Slocum's direction. Huge chunks of the wooden table disappeared with each explosion as he huddled behind it. The men were moving down the hallway even before the wooden splinters settled.

Before the last bullet slammed into the table and the smoke from the gunfire drifted away, the men were taking up strategic positions behind the bar and tables and behind huge wooden posts, trying to pin Slocum down.

"Is that you, Slocum?" Steppe called out, somewhere to Slocum's left. With the high ceilings, sounds carried differently. Slocum could have been ten inches, ten feet, or ten yards away.

Slocum said nothing.

"Behind the table, boss," said one of the poker players behind the bar.

"Get him, Pete," Steppe growled.

Slocum heard heavy footsteps headed in his direction. Slocum knew the move. He'd have to expose himself in order to get the man walking toward him, leaving him vulnerable. Slocum reloaded quickly as the footsteps approached.

Clutching both six-shooters, Slocum jumped up and fired both, spitting lead in every direction. There was no return fire. One shot—maybe more, though Slocum had no time to check—took a fair-sized chunk of Pete's face off. The poor bastard went flying back into the bar and plummeted into the sawdust-covered floor.

Slocum knew he had to get out from behind the table. Through a bullet hole in the table, he could see one of the poker players give a couple of sawed-off twelve-gauge shotguns to some of his friends. There was just enough light filtering through some boarded-up alley windows for him to see faint silhouettes of his enemy.

Slocum duck-walked to the edge of the table, then bounded out from behind it, rolled on the sawdust, and dived behind another table just as Steppe and his men opened fire, blasting the table he'd been hiding behind. Between them they left a gaping hole in the center.

Steppe kicked the remains of the table over. Slocum wasn't there.

"What makes him so damn restless?" Slocum heard Steppe mutter angrily.

Slocum jumped up and pumped lead in a steady twelve-shot stream. He caught the man next to Steppe twice in the spine. Steppe and the other two hit the floor and started scampering in different directions. One of them changed his mind, leveled his twelve-gauge at Slocum, and squeezed off a shot.

Slocum felt himself being knocked backwards, as though someone had yanked his left shoulder. His shoulder was on fire, and he could already feel the warm blood trickling down his arm. The guy hadn't scored a direct hit, Slocum knew at once. If he had, half of his neck would be gone. Still, it was close enough.

"Got the bastard!" someone yelled.

Slocum lay sprawled on the floor, his back against the wall. The impact of the shot had knocked both guns out of his hands. One was within reaching distance. He struggled with his good arm to reach for it, but the pain in his shoulder was paralyzing. The shot had taken out a hefty piece of flesh.

Steppe and the other two walked toward Slocum, sawed-off shotguns clenched firmly in their hands.

Slocum clutched his shoulder. Blood oozed out between his fingers. He looked Steppe square in the eye.

"Had enough?" he asked Steppe.

Steppe leveled his shotgun a few inches from Slocum's head.

"The papers said you went home," Steppe said.

"Not likely," Slocum said.

Steppe cocked the trigger of his rifle. The men on either side of him did likewise. They were tough mugs, and Slocum had killed several of their pals.

"When you see my father in hell," Steppe said, his voice dripping hatred, "turn up the heat on him."

A shot rang out behind them. The mug to Steppe's left arched his back, dropped his shotgun, then fell where he stood.

Slocum looked up and watched as Dopey Bennie appeared behind them out of the murky darkness. Before he could even fire again, Steppe wheeled around and let loose with both barrels. Dopey Bennie took them in the middle of the belly. He went flying backwards, most of his stomach a bloody pulp, into some tables and chairs.

"Bastards!" Davie Liebowitz cried, stepping out from behind a wooden Indian in the corner. He started firing blindly from hell to breakfast, two of his errant shots finding a home in the last mug's face. He crumpled on top of his dead friend.

Steppe turned his sights on Davie and fired. Davie slipped behind the wooden Indian again, but not quick enough. He took one in the leg, right above the knee. He bounced off the bogus Cherokee and fell hard.

Slocum gritted his teeth and jerked himself forward just far enough to grab his gun. Before he could raise it though, Steppe had wheeled back around, the shotgun pointed at Slocum.

"This is all your fault," Steppe said, and squeezed the trigger.

The empty click seemed muffled in the gunsmoke. Steppe's eyes widened, almost comically, Slocum thought, in surprised shock.

Slocum pointed his gun at Steppe and said, "Drop it, unless you want a third nostril."

Steppe dropped the shotgun. "I suppose you want me to raise my arms above my head," he said.

"You suppose right."

Steppe did. "You gonna kill me?"

"Ain't decided yet," Slocum said, feeling increasingly light-headed. He'd lost a lot of blood and was losing more.

"I can wait," Steppe said and smiled. Even in the faint light, he could see how pale Slocum looked. A cold sweat had broken out on his forehead.

Slocum had never killed an unarmed man, and was trying hard to decide whether to bend his rules this one time. His goal of a trial in Brushwood Gulch seemed to fade with each ounce of blood that trickled out of him. Death seemed very real now, and he'd be damned if Steppe was going to walk away again.

Slocum cocked the trigger, his hand shaking badly. He was fuzzy-headed, his brain made of molasses. The last thing Slocum remembered was seeing Steppe kick the gun out of his hand.

Damn, he thought, and plunged headlong into a pool of darkness.

19

Two weeks later, Slocum was released from St. Mary's Hospital, deemed fit enough by doctors to go home.

True to form, Flannery and his men arrived after the shooting was over, having been informed of Steppe's whereabouts by a waterfront rogue named Spider O'Toole who owed Flannery a favor or two. Flannery knew that somehow Slocum would find his way there as well, and swooped down on the saloon just as Steppe was about to ventilate the stubborn lawman.

Slocum and Davie Liebowitz were rushed to St. Mary's, while Steppe was rushed to the prison stockade on Bayard Street. Davie recovered quickly, gave Slocum his regards, and went home where he complained endlessly about the rotten hospital food. Dopey Bennie, Slocum was told by Flannery, was given a hero's send-off.

What about Sally, Slocum had asked. Had she gotten a Christian burial?

She had, Flannery assured him, paid for by the department.

For a week after the blazing shootout, Slocum was the toast of New York. Wildly exaggerated accounts of it were plastered on the front pages of every newspaper in town. There was even talk of a John Slocum Day and a parade down Fourteenth Street, both of which Slocum nixed. He just wanted to get better and leave this lunatic asylum of a city.

"All aboard for the Chicago Limited, departing in ten minutes on track thirteen," the conductor wailed.

Once again, Slocum sat on the hard wooden bench, only this time surrounded by thirty policemen. Flannery wasn't taking any more chances this time, he told Slocum. Steppe was safely tucked away in a heavily guarded cell in the Tombs and it was there he would stay until his trial for murder and a host of other crimes. "Don't worry," Flannery had said. "It's the gallows for him, and ours are as good as any in Colorado."

"Just hand him over to me and you can save the city the price of a trial and hanging," Slocum suggested. Flannery turned him down.

"You ready to go, Slocum?" Flannery asked now.

"I reckon," Slocum said, and stood. Though he was pretty much healed, he still had his right arm in a sling.

Stumpy Malarkey weaseled his way through the crowd of cops.

"Hold on there," he cried. "I didn't say me farewells."

Stumpy came forward and handed Slocum a bottle of whiskey. "Something to quench your thirst along the way," he said.

Slocum gladly accepted the bottle. "Thanks, Stumpy. You take care now and give my best to the wife."

"Sad she is to see you go," Stumpy said. "Try to stay out of trouble. If you can't, at least leave me out of it."

"Will do, partner," Slocum said as Flannery led him toward the train track.

"Got your ticket?" Flannery asked.

"Yeah," Slocum said. "Seat forty-three, compartment nine."

"Good," Flannery said.

"Don't suppose you want to reconsider and hand Steppe over to me," Slocum said.

"Can't do it," Flannery said. "Sorry."

"Then I'll be back," Slocum said.

"And I'll be waiting," Flannery said.

"Last call for the Chicago Limited," the conductor cried. "With stops in Philadelphia, Harrisburg, Pittsburgh, and Toledo! All aboard on track thirteen!"

They walked to the train, surrounded by policemen.

"You did all right, Slocum, for a country boy," Flannery said. "Be gone with you now."

Slocum extended his hand. Flannery took it.

"Sorry for the shiners," Slocum said. "Thanks for saving my life and shit."

Slocum hopped up the three steps onto the train. Seconds later it started chugging slowly out of the station.

"Remember, Slocum," Flannery called as the train picked up speed. "Next time I shoot you on sight."

"Gives me something to look forward to," Slocum called back.

Slocum ambled through the passenger cars looking for his seat until a Negro porter approached him.

"You-all John Slocum?" the porter asked.

Slocum nodded.

"Den follow me, please," the porter said. Slocum followed the porter, who led Slocum to his seat by the window.

In the seat next to his, Samuel Steppe sat handcuffed to

the armrest. A huge red ribbon was tied around his chest with a note that read "Take him and stay the hell away from me. Best regards, Flannery."

"Well, well, well," Slocum said with a grin. "What do we have here?"

Steppe gave him a sour look, his face contorted with indignant rage.

Slocum plunked down in the seat next to his prisoner. The porter reappeared with a red velvet box, which he handed to Slocum.

"Another gift from Mr. Flannery," the porter said.

Inside was a brand new Colt with another note that read, "You might be needing this." Slocum examined the shiny gun, spinning the barrel a few times as the train stopped lurching and settled into steady motion.

"What happens now?" Steppe asked him.

"What do you think?" Slocum said. "You stand trial for murder in Brushwood Gulch."

"You'll never get me back there," Steppe said. "I'll try to kill you the first chance I get."

"Wouldn't have much respect for you if you didn't," Slocum said. "But you won't get the chance. Besides, I found you this time, and I'd find you again."

Slocum flipped open the cylinder of the Colt and started loading it. "You see, Mr. Samuel Steppe, you're dealing with Sheriff John Slocum, friend to those who deserve it, and enemy to those who don't. Upholder of justice, tireless defender of the innocent, punisher of the wicked and guilty. Bringing justice to these United States and—"

With his free arm, Steppe slammed Slocum in the mouth with his elbow. Slocum's head bounced off the window, leaving a six-inch crack in the thick glass.

"If I got to listen to your bullshit all the way to

Colorado," Steppe said, "do me a favor and kill me now."

Slocum rubbed his cheek and tried to clear his head. The train continued picking up speed.

"You know, Sammy," Slocum said, a bit sobered, "this could be the beginning of a beautiful friendship."

The wolf loped through the brush, moving soundlessly over the sandy soil. From time to time it stopped, testing the air, scanning its surroundings, listening. It was an old wolf, had grown old because of its caution, because of listening, watching, never showing itself. There once had been many wolves in the area, but most were gone now, most dead, killed by men with rifles, and traps, and poison. This particular wolf had long ago learned to avoid man, or anything that smelled of man. And it had survived.

It was late spring; the sagebrush still showed some green. The wolf had been eating well lately, many animals browsed on that green, and the wolf browsed on the animals, the smaller ones, the ones he could catch by himself. There were no longer any wolf packs to pull down bigger game: deer, antelope. Life was now a succession of small meals, barely mouthfuls.

The wolf was thirsty. A quarter of a mile ahead a patch of thicker green showed. A water hole. The wolf could smell the water. It increased its pace, loping along, bouncing on still-springy legs, tongue lolling from its mouth, yellow eyes alert.

A thicket of willows some fifteen feet high, grew up on the far side of the water hole. The wolf gave them a cursory scan. It raised its nose, its main warning system, and could smell only water, willows, and mud.

It was late enough in the season for the water hole to have shrunk to a scummy puddle, no more than a foot deep and twenty feet across. In winter, when the rains came, the water formed a small lake. One more look around, then the wolf dropped its muzzle, pushed scum aside, and lapped slowly at the water. After half a minute the wolf raised its head again, turning it from side to side, nervous. The water had claimed its attention for a dangerously long time.

Suddenly, the wolf froze. Perhaps the horse had made a small movement. Horses do not like the company of wolves, yet this one had stood motionless while the wolf approached, held so by the man on its back. The wolf saw him then, the man, blending into the willow thicket, mounted, sitting perfectly motionless.

A moment's stab of fear, the wolf's muscles bunching, ready to propel him away. But the wolf did not run. Ears pricked high, it stood still, looking straight at the man, sensing that he meant him no harm. Sensing, in its wolf's brain, an affinity with this particular man.

Wolf and man continued to look at one another for perhaps a half a minute. Then the wolf, with great dignity, turned, and loped away. Within seconds it had vanished into the brush.

The man did not move until he could no longer see the wolf. Then, with gentle pressure from his knees, he urged the horse out of the willows, down toward the water hole, let it drink again. The horse had been drinking earlier, head down, legs splayed out, when the man had first seen the wolf, or rather, seen movement, about a quarter of a mile away, a flicker of gray gliding through the chaparral. He was not quite sure why he'd backed his horse into the willows, why he'd quieted the animal down as the wolf approached. Perhaps he wanted to see if it could be done, if he could become invisible to the wolf. Because if he could do that, he should be able to become invisible to anything.

The wind had been from the wolf's direction. The horse's hoofs had crushed some water plants at the edge of the pool; they gave off a strong odor, masking the man's scent, masking the horse's. A trick old Jedadiah had shown him, all those years ago . . . let nature herself conceal you.

He'd watched as the wolf approached the water hole, made one last cursory check of its surroundings, then began to drink. A big, gaunt old fellow. The man wondered how the hell it had survived. Damned stockmen had done their best to exterminate every wolf within five hundred miles. Exterminate everything except their cows.

He was aware of the moment the wolf sensed his presence, knew it would happen an instant before it actually did. He watched the wolf's head rise, its body tense. But he knew that it would not run. Or rather, sensed it. No, more than that . . . it was as if he and the wolf shared a single mind, were the same species. Brothers. The man smiled. Why not? Both he and the wolf shared a way of life . . . they were both the hunter and the hunted.

The wolf was gone now, the moment over, and the man, pulling his horse's head up from the water before it drank too much, left the pool and rode out into the brush. And as he rode, anyone able to watch from some celestial vantage point would have noticed that he travelled pretty much as

the wolf had travelled, almost invisible in the brush, just
flickers of movement as he guided his horse over a route
that would expose him least, avoiding high ground, never
riding close to clumps of brush that were too thick to see
into, places that might conceal other men.

He rode until about an hour before dark, then he began
to look for a place to make camp for the night. He found
it a quarter of an hour later, a small depression surrounded
by fairly thick chaparral, but not so thick that he could not
see out through it.

Dismounting, he quickly stripped the gear from his
horse, the bedroll and saddlebags coming off first, laid
neatly together near the place where he knew he would
build a small fire. He drew his two rifles, the big Sharps
and the lighter Winchester, from their saddle scabbards,
and propped them against a bush, within easy reach. The
saddle came off next; he heard his horse sigh with relief
when he loosened the girth.

Reaching into his saddlebags, the man pulled out a
hackamore made of soft, braided leather. Working with
the ease that comes from doing the same thing dozens
of times, he slipped the bit and bridle off his horse, and
replaced it with the hackamore. Now, the horse would be
able to graze as it wished, without a mouthful of iron
bit in the way. More importantly, if there was danger, if
the man had to leave immediately, he would have some
kind of head stall already on his horse. When trouble
came, speed was essential, thus the hackamore, and the
style of his saddle, a center-fire rig, less stable than a
double rig, but easy to throw on a horse when you were
in a hurry.

The man fastened a long lead rope to the hackamore,
tied the free end to a stout bush, then left his horse free
to move where it wanted. He allowed himself a minute

to sink down onto the sandy ground, studying the area around him, alert, but also aware of the peacefulness of the place. There was no sound at all except the soft movement of the warm breeze through the bushes, and, a hundred yards away, a single bird, singing its heart out.

In the midst of this quiet the man was aware of the workings of his mind. He was comfortable with his mind, liked to let it roam free, liked to watch the way it worked. He had learned over the years that most other men were uneasy with their minds, tried to blot them out with liquor or religion.

His gaze wandered over to his horse. To the hackamore. He remembered the original Spanish word for halter . . . *jaquima*, altered now by the Anglo cowboy. Through his reading, and he read a great deal, the man had discovered that many of the words the Western horseman used were of Spanish origin, usually changed almost beyond recognition. When the first American cowboys came out West, they learned their trade from the original Western settlers, the Spanish *vaqueros*. Matchless horsemen, those Spaniards, especially out in California. God they could ride!

When the Anglos moved into Texas, it was the local Mexicans who'd taught them how to handle cattle in those wide open spaces. Yet, he knew that most cowboys were totally unaware of the roots of the words they used every day. Not this man. He liked to think about words, about meanings, mysteries. He had an unquenchable hunger to learn.

And at the moment, a more basic hunger. There was movement off to his left; a jackrabbit, one of God's stupider creatures, was hopping toward him. The rabbit stopped about ten yards away, then stood up on its hind legs so that it could more easily study this strange-smelling object. Rabbit and man were both immobile for several seconds, watching one another, then the man moved, one smooth motion, the pistol on his hip now in his hand, the hammer snicking back, the roar of a shot racketing around the little depression.

Peering through a big cloud of white gunsmoke, the man thought at first he had missed; he could not see the rabbit. But then he did see it, or what was left of it, lying next to a bush a yard from where it had been sitting when he'd fired. He got up, went over to the dead rabbit. The big .45 caliber bullet had not left much of the head or front quarters, but that didn't matter. The hind quarters were where the meat was.

It took him less than five minutes to skin and gut the rabbit. He methodically picked out the big parasitic worms that lived beneath the rabbit's scruffy hide, careful not to smash them, and ruin the meat. Ugly things. It took another fifteen minutes to get a fire going, and while the fire burned down to hot coals, the man whittled a spit out of a springy manzanilla branch, and ran it through the rabbit.

It was dark before the rabbit was cooked. After seeing those worms, the man wanted to make sure the meat was done all the way through. He ate slowly, trying not to burn his fingers. For dessert he fished a small can of peaches out of his saddlebags. His only drink was warm, brakish water from his canteen. But he considered the meal a success, not so much because of the bill of fare, but because of the elegance of his surroundings: the pristine cleanness of the sandy ground on which he sat, the perfume of the chaparral, the broad band of the Milky Way arching overhead, undimmed.

Yeah, he thought, pretty damned beautiful. He scratched his chin through a week's unshaven bristle. And reflected